SUMMER SHIVERS

SUMMERS IN SEASIDE COLLABORATION

DENISE WELLS

Cover Design by: Amy Queau at QDesign Covers and Premades

Editing by: Rachel Melignano

Proofreading by: Krissy M at Author Bunnies, Author Services

Formatting by: Rdhdwriter

PR by: Enticing Journey Book Promotions

Published in the United States of America

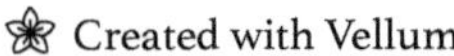 Created with Vellum

PRAISE FOR OTHER BOOKS BY DENISE

I loved this book because of the sassy banter between the main couple, and the writing style is quite entertaining.

— AMAZON REVIEWER

This was a fantastic read. The storyline has just enough angst and drama to keep it interesting without becoming frustrating or over the top.

— AMAZON REVIEWER

I loved this story it was great all the way through!

— AMAZON REVIEWER

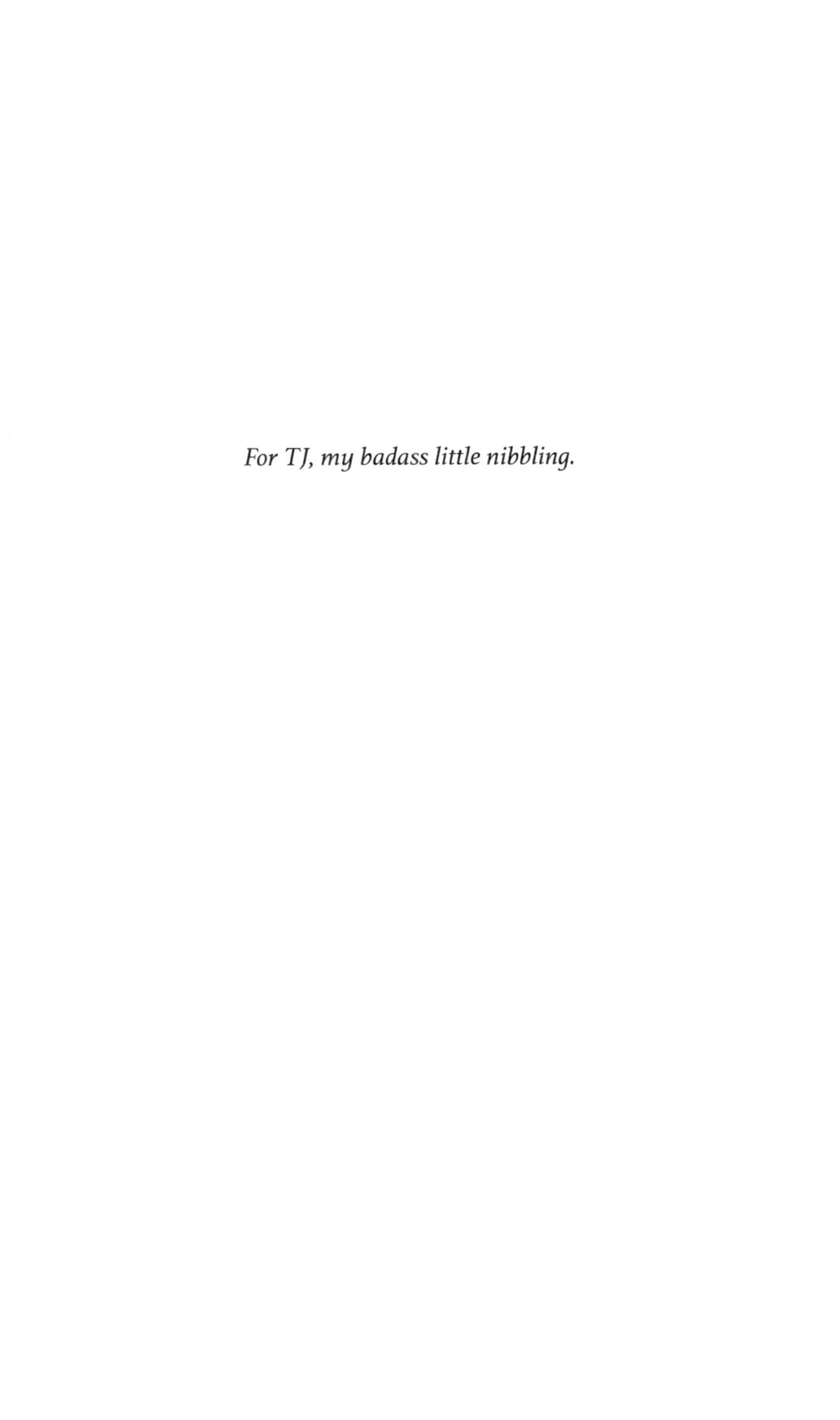

For TJ, my badass little nibbling.

Sometimes when you're in a dark place, you think you've been buried. But you've actually been planted.

— ANONYMOUS

SUMMER SHIVERS

GENEVIEVE
I didn't kill my husband.
At least I don't think I did.
But all evidence points to me and I can't remember a thing about that night.
There are only two people in my life who would inherently trust I'm innocent. One of them just died.
The other is my ex Tyler Presley; who I still have feelings for.
What kind of monster mourns one man while trying to seduce another?
Me. I'm that kind of monster.

TYLER
Genevieve Daniels thinks she can call me, four years after decimating my heart, and I'll ride up like some chump on my white horse to save her.
Not a chance.
Still, I'll play right into her game of seduction. If only to mess with her. Show her what it's like to crumble.

Am I that much of a monster?
Yes. Yes, I am.

1

Genevieve

"How was that?" my husband, Harrison, asks, rolling off me to collapse on his side of the bed, still breathing heavily from his orgasm.

"It was good." I sigh, trying to sound satisfied.

If I don't, he'll be upset.

I didn't come. I rarely do. But it makes me happy when my husband does. Sometimes that happiness comes through in my voice, and I can play it off like that after-sex glow.

I don't think this is one of those times.

"Yeah?" He turns to face me. "What part?"

I hate when he asks me that question. As though I was taking notes on his performance and can give him a report back at the end.

"Uh—that part where you swivel your hips was really good."

"Which time?" His hand rests on his chest as it rises and falls with each inhale and exhale.

"I don't remember the exact time that you did that. I was kind of preoccupied. You know, making love to you." I turn my head to face him, forcing a smile to my face.

He frowns in return. "What about when I put your ankles over my shoulders?"

His constant need for reassurance can be exhausting. And even though I know his insecurity is one hundred percent my fault there are some days, like today, where I just don't want to play into it.

But I still do.

"I loved that part," I enthuse.

His body stiffens.

I realize my mistake at once. It's not that I wasn't paying attention during sex. Actually, that's exactly what it was. Sometimes I just check out and other times I pretend he's someone else.

"I didn't put your ankles over my shoulders." His voice is cold.

"Are you sure?"

"Of course, I'm sure. Don't you think I know exactly what I was doing the whole time I was doing it?"

I have no response to that.

We lie next to one another in awkward silence. His anger radiates off him in waves. I know what's coming next and I don't want to deal with it. Not tonight. Just once I'd like to go through an evening of sex without this coming up.

"You were thinking about him, weren't you?" His eyes narrow.

"I was thinking about you." My voice sounds flat. Even I don't believe myself as I say it. How can I expect him to?

"Bullshit you were thinking about me." He sits up, the sheet falling to his waist. He's in good shape for a man his age. A man who is twenty years senior to my twenty-eight. I reach out to touch his chest to soothe him, but he jerks away before I can make contact.

He's handsome—my husband—wealthy, intelligent, charismatic. It helps my state of mind to remind myself of all his good qualities when he gets like this. All the reasons why I agreed to marry him. Because nothing throws me into a downward emotional spiral more than fighting with Harrison. I continue to remind myself that I made the right decision marrying a man I don't desire. Usually, it reassures me. Today it just leaves me feeling empty and unfulfilled.

"Maybe I should feel relieved that you still didn't come even though you were thinking about him."

"Harrison..."

"Don't, Genevieve." He sighs, running his hands through his hair.

"You know I enjoy being with you—being intimate with you," I say to appease him.

He stares at me, eyes blinking rapidly. "You *enjoy* it?"

"It's not about the orgasm," I continue, trying to make him understand. "It's about being together and loving one another and that's what we do. The orgasm is just a side component. It doesn't matter."

"Well, I guess it's good having a baby doesn't rely on your orgasm or you'd never let me touch you." He gets up and heads to the bathroom.

"That's not fair, Harrison. And it's not true!" I yell after him.

"It's absolutely fucking true. You can't stand it when I touch you. Every time you wish it was him. Just admit it, Genevieve. Admit, you still love him!" he yells from the other room.

Harrison's statement hangs in the air between us, like an albatross around my neck. He comes back into the room and begins to mutter to himself as he paces back and forth along the side of the bed. His arms gesticulate above his head as he moves, casting shadows on the bedroom wall behind him mimicking claws descending or fangs protruding. A shadow puppet monster or something equally hideous that would have terrified me as a child but amuse me as an adult.

"You know I do," I admit softly. "A part of me always will. But I'm with you now, and we're together, trying for a family. I'm happy with that."

The *him* Harrison is referring to is my ex, Tyler Presley. The love of my life if I'm being honest. The only man to ever make me come. The man who thought it more important to put his own life in danger than to stay and live our happily ever after with me. One who continued to break pieces of my heart when he chose work over me time and again until I couldn't take it any longer.

"Well, I'm not happy with that." Harrison stops pacing long enough to face and stare me down. His chest still heaving, though now out of anger instead of arousal. His penis hangs limply between his legs. "Not anymore."

"What does that mean?"

He ignores my question, instead disappearing into his walk-in closet.

"Harrison?" I call after him. He emerges wearing swim trunks.

"Are you—"

"How can you just admit that to me, your husband, so easily?" he interrupts asking about my feelings for Ty. Which, in the beginning of our relationship, he swore would never be a problem. Something he has most definitely changed his mind about in the past couple of years as I've continued to not 'get over it.'

"Why are you acting like this is something new?" I counter.

"Why haven't you gotten over him?" he throws back at me. "We've been married twice as long as you were even with that guy."

I don't have an answer to that. It's like asking why my old black and white checkered Vans are still my favorite shoes, even though I've got a closet full of designer, red-soled high heels, the worth of which could probably buy a small house in most areas of the country.

I shrug as my response.

I care deeply for Harrison, but I'll never feel for him the way I (still) do for Tyler. With Tyler it was like he was the very oxygen I needed to breathe. If he was away for any length of time without contact, I would slowly shrivel up and start to die. Which is what I would have done after Ty and I broke up if Harrison hadn't saved me.

A breakup I'm still not over. Even though it was four years ago, and he and I were only together half that time. Tyler, the man I thought I'd spend the rest of my life with, growing a family together. The father of my stillborn baby— a baby who would have been three and a half in two months. My mind never quite able to stop counting the days, weeks, months since I lost her. The age she would be today. How long it's been since she was conceived. A pang of longing scissors through me. Longing for the baby that never happened and for the man who helped create it.

"Why aren't I enough?" Harrison's voice cracks, breaking up my thoughts and piercing at my heart. A cloud of despair falls over his face that makes me want to wrap him in a hug and never let him go.

I open my mouth to respond, not even yet knowing what

I want to say. He holds up a hand to stop me from talking, even though I haven't begun.

Harrison knows he and I will never have the passion that Tyler and I did. We spent a lot of time together as employer and assistant before we were married. It's actually how we met. And that time together helped to develop a strong friendship. Which is all I'll ever feel for him. Though that same friendship, for him, quickly turned to love.

"Why can't you be satisfied with the man you have instead of yearning for the one who doesn't want you?"

The question stings even though the words ring true. Again, I have no response. At least not one that will help him to feel better. Despite that, the phrase tickles at my brain, as though I've heard it before but can't remember.

Until I do.

"Did you just quote the main character from one of your last chapters?" I ask, furious with myself for not recognizing what he was doing.

He doesn't even look ashamed. "The words aren't any less true if I did."

My husband, Harrison Daniels, is a world-renowned, chart topping—hell chart-breaking—thriller/horror writer. He's written/co-written more than 200 novels in his (so far) twenty-five-year career. Most of which have been New York Times, Wall Street Journal, and/or USA Today bestselling novels. I've been his assistant for the last six years and have read pretty much everything he's ever written.

That said, this wouldn't be the first time he's worked a scene into our marriage or vice versa. He likes to hear the words said aloud, but in realistic settings. He says that's how he knows they ring true.

Which is why he'll pick a fight, like the one tonight, that has originated from a scene. Or one like last week, about where we should vacation this year, that he can tailor into a scene. I'm more used to it now, being manipulated like this, so much so, I shouldn't even be surprised.

But I am.

He continues, "Let me and the baby we want to have be your future. Let go of him and the past."

Harrison and I are trying to have a baby. Not in a fertility drug or in vitro kind of way, but in an *if it happens, it happens* kind of way.

Because even though all my dreams of my life included Ty as the father to my children, I still want them. And Ty is no longer an option. Because when I gave him an ultimatum, he didn't cave. And I didn't even know I was pregnant then, or I may not have given it.

Finding out I was pregnant after the break up is why, when Harrison convinced me to marry him, I went along with it. For him, it was his dream come true. For me it was a solid foundation in which to raise a child whose father would never know they existed.

I've been honest with Harrison every step of the way, about my feelings and my lack of sexual attraction to him. He still gets offended when I don't climax. Which is how fights like tonight's start.

Harrison is right to accuse me of still being in love with Tyler.

I am.

"Are you going to answer me?" he asks, interrupting my thoughts again.

"What was the question?"

He throws his hands up in disgust. "I'm going for a swim. Don't wait up."

So, I don't. Instead, going about my nightly skin care routine, followed by another glass of wine and a sleeping pill. While I wait for the combination to kick in, I grab my e-reader and pull up my favorite book of erotic short stories for women, which opens right to my favorite story.

A WOMAN IS RIDING a crowded subway. She's wearing a short skirt with a matching jacket. Maybe on her way home from work, that part is never clear. She gets pinned between a grab pole in front of her and a man behind her. She can feel that he's strong and he smells good. He grabs onto her hip as the subway sways, helping to steady her. His hand moves down her leg and under the edge of her skirt. Her breath holds waiting to see what he'll do next. He toys with the edge of her garter and stocking, running his fingers along the lace edge. Inching closer to her center, but taking his time doing it.

She waits in anticipation.

When he pushes her panties aside with his fingers, she's soaked.

"Is that for me?" he grumbles in her ear.

She nods, unable to speak.

I GRAB my vibrator from the nightstand drawer and turn it on at a medium setting.

THE SUBWAY sways some back and forth, the motion sensual, pushing his fingers in and out of her pussy.

"You want my dick?"

"Yes," she whispers.

The man plunges his dick inside her, stealing her breath.

She cries out.

"Easy, doll," the man commands softly before biting her neck.

He reaches a hand around to push her clit down, letting it rub against the edge of his cock as he lets the sway of the subway move them languidly back and forth.

"Goddamn, you feel good." The timbre of his voice makes her shiver and within seconds she's coming harder than she ever has in her life.

He buries his face in the back of her neck, groaning as he comes inside her. She feels him pull out and situate himself back in his pants. He smooths her skirt back into place as he says, "Same time tomorrow, doll," and disappears.

I CRY out Tyler's name as my own climax takes over, leaving me exhausted enough to sleep, a satisfied smile on my face.

2

———————

Tyler

I hate being in Seaside, Oregon again. The whole goddamn city makes me jumpy.

Way too many bad memories live here.

Place I grew up, barely raised by a narcissistic mom and absentee dad.

Where my heart was ripped to shreds by the woman I still love.

And my brother was killed by a man I've still not found. Not even after looking for over four years.

A death ruled a suicide. I don't buy it. No way my brother would've offed himself. He wasn't that guy. Now I spend my free time tracking down anything I can about his last living days. That, and I come get drunk at his grave. Same time every year—anniversary of his death. Catch him up on what's been going on in my life, make tasteless jokes about him just lying around wasting his away.

Like now, I come in the day before, make my way downtown to drink myself into a stupor, then pass out in some cheap motel room close by.

I was already feelin' restless before I got here. In between assignments from my buddy's company—Alpha Team Security. Knew him from special forces. Mack Murphy. He was in the FBI for a while, got fed up with the bullshit and left. Now he runs his own company based out of Seattle, Washington. I joined up with him and his partner about four years ago.

Shortly after my brother died.

And my girl broke my heart.

And my stint in rehab.

And the eleven surgeries that couldn't put my knee back together.

Stories for another time.

I don't love Seattle, but it's how I can pop down to Seaside easily and keep searching for clues.

I check in to the Budget Inn before making my way down South Columbia Street toward my bar of choice: Beach Club on North Downing. A five-minute walk that always seems longer because half of it's on residential streets. City makes no fucking sense.

Probably why I can't get any information on my brother's death. Cops have been no help at all. Police file and coroner's report disappeared ages ago—supposedly never even entered in the system. Even my brother's best friend, Alissa (Al for short), a computer hacking genius, can't track them down. Which means they are nowhere on the web. Highly suspect if you ask me.

Last time I lived here was with the girl of my dreams. I was even going to propose—fuck, had the perfect ring just hadn't found the perfect time. Girl deserved something magical, you know? She could brag to all her girlfriends, make them jealous as fuck.

I'm not a romantic guy. It was not easy tryin' to come up with something. Problem is when you start setting unrealistic expectations for yourself, reality keeps pushing them further and further down the line of life.

I get ready to pop the question, my brother dies. Supposed overdose from a guy who wouldn't even light up a joint. His body was his temple. That guy who put nothing but lean proteins and vegetables in his body all the time. Stayed hydrated and took vitamins. Drove me fucking crazy.

Still, I loved him, his death shook me to the core.

So, when we got the lead on the kingpin pushing the drug that killed my brother, I had to go. Re-join my team, track him down. Problem was, I'd promised my girl that last mission was my last. That anything going forward would be low-key contract work. She didn't like me *risking my life like that*, her words, not mine. I loved her enough, didn't mind. That much.

But, spinning up to track that worthless-piece-of-drug-pushing-shit down was a no-brainer. And I couldn't tell my girl why I had to go. Clearance and all that. She knew my job was secret, always gonna be stuff I couldn't share with her. Still, she fucking gave me an ultimatum—'*if you go, so do I.*'

Swallowed my pride, begged her to wait. She begged me to stay. Swore it would be my last mission, for real. Problem is, you make the same promise one too many times and it becomes meaningless.

I spun up, she moved out.

Last I heard she'd married her douche bag of a boss and moved to Lake Oswego. Got a house here in Seaside, one in Seattle too, and probably a bunch of other places. He's a rich douche bag. Writes all these simpleton crime solving stories for the masses. Three-page chapters with everything ending on a cliffhanger. Plots with serial killers who keep getting away with it.

Not that I would ever read that shit. Too far-fetched from a law enforcement perspective. I'd be lying if I said it wasn't vexing *that's* who she chose after me.

I had Al check up on her—she seemed happy. Hate her for breaking my heart, but a small part of me wants to know hers is still okay. Probably better this way, my life went to shit after that last run.

Fast forward through multiple surgeries, a stint in rehab, medical discharge from special forces, and a permanent limp on my left side to where I am today. Fuck of it is, we didn't even catch the guy like we thought we would.

That's when I hooked up with Mack. Started doing what I'm doing now. The rest, as they say, is history.

I pull open the door to Beach Bar. Not too crowded, not too quiet. Grab a seat at the bar and proceed to drink myself into a stupor. As is customary on the anniversary of my brother's death.

3

____

Genevieve

I wake with a start. But not sure why as I open my eyes. My alarm didn't go off, there's no sunlight shining through the black-out shades in our bedroom, and I'm alone in our bed so Harrison's flopping around was also not the culprit.

His side of the bed remains relatively untouched.

Figures he'd sulk all night and sleep in another room. I hate it when he gets in these moods.

I take my time stretching before getting out of bed and am surprised to see it's almost eight o'clock in the morning. My alarm must not have been set, which would explain why it didn't go off and I'm waking an hour later than usual. I'm also surprised that Harrison didn't wake me up.

Or bring me coffee.

The top of my nightstand remains bare where a mug usually sits.

Even when he's mad at me, Harrison will bring me a cup of coffee first thing and leave it on my nightstand. I have a small mug heater that keeps it warm until I wake up. Not that I sleep that late, mind you, just that Harrison gets up that early. That should have happened almost two hours ago, by now.

Luckily, I don't have anything planned for this morning that I've missed. But I think Harrison has a phone appointment with his attorney, Grant, later. I put on a robe and make my way to the kitchen. Two things I must have before I can start my day. Coffee and a shower.

Huh.

No coffee made in the kitchen either. Harrison must either be really pissed, or he's sleeping in. His office door is still shut, my guess is he's probably in there licking his wounds. He takes our discussions about Ty so personally.

I grab a K-cup and make myself a mug the new-fangled way. Harrison hates it and prefers the taste of a pot that's been brewed, but I think it's great for something quick. He says the sound of the maker spitting coffee into the carafe is meditative for him.

The Keurig beeps that it's finished. In roughly one-tenth of the time a whole pot would have taken, I note with satisfaction. I'm tempted to knock on his office door as I head back to my bathroom to take a shower but decide to let him sleep a while longer, just in case. There's nothing crankier than a pouting Harrison who didn't get enough sleep.

ONE HOUR LATER

I head to the backyard leisurely strolling through the gardens to get to the pool. Stopping to admire the sparkling blue water in the morning sunlight.

Something's not right.

It takes a moment for my brain to catch up with what I'm seeing.

Harrison is floating face down in the endless pool.

Is he still swimming?

"Harrison?" I call out to him.

He's not moving.

It takes another moment for my brain to digest that.

Along with the slightest tinge of pink surrounding the back of his head.

Is that blood?

"Oh my god, Harrison!"

My coffee cup falls to the ground, the hot brew splashing my skin as it goes, the mug shatters into hundreds of pieces. I move forward, barely feeling the nicks of the ceramic or the burn of the liquid as I jump into action. Jumping into the pool, I make my way toward him, grabbing hold around his chest, and pulling him toward the edge. I'm not strong enough to push him up and out.

I look around frantic.

The steps between the pool and spa.

I pull him there and realize I can try to roll him on to one of the main steps between the two. I get him onto his back; vacant, wide-open eyes stare back at me. His mouth is agape, water trickling out the edges and down his jaw. A bluish hue colors his wrinkled and pruned skin.

"Harrison?" I whimper.

I don't know CPR outside of what I've seen on TV: hitting the chest and breathing into the mouth; both of which I try to no avail. He doesn't turn his head and cough up water like in the movies. I rush to the pool house, my wet T-shirt and shorts dripping and sticking to my skin.

"9-1-1, what's your emergency?"

"Hello." Words are hardly forming in my mouth. "I need help please hurry."

"Okay, can you tell me what's happened?"

"It's my husband, he won't wake up."

"And where is your husband?"

"In the pool."

"What's your name?"

"Genevieve. Daniels."

"And what's your address, Genevieve."

"Please hurry."

"Can you give me your location?"

I give the dispatcher my address, begging them again to send help. My teeth chatter and my body shivers in the cool morning breeze.

"I-I... n-need to get back to him," I stutter.

"Where are you now, can you bring the phone with you?"

Harrison doesn't like being alone. Unless he's writing, then he demands total solitude. "Oh, yes. I'm on a cordless phone."

"Are there any weapons at your house, Genevieve?"

"What? No."

"How old is your husband?"

"Are you sending help?"

"Help is on the way. I'm sorry for the questions, but the more information I have the better it is for the EMTs once they get there. How old is your husband?"

"Uh, he's forty-eight."

"Any health issues?"

"No, he's in great health."

"You said he won't wake up. Is he breathing?"

"I don't think so, no."

"Okay, did you move him or attempt to resuscitate?"

"I tried to push him out of the pool, but I couldn't. I've got him halfway on the stair now. It's an endless pool with an attached spa. I don't know CPR."

"That's okay. EMT's will be there soon. Can you tell me the color of your house, and where the pool is on the property?"

"Uh, if they come in the driveway, it's a tan house, like beige, and if they come in the driveway and park by the fountain, they can just head through the gardens on the right to the back of the house."

"That's very helpful, Genevieve, thank you."

"Will they be able to get in? Should I open the gate?"

"Definitely, if there's a gate at the entrance, please open it now."

I rush to the control panel to open the gate remotely, before returning to Harrison. "Oh god," I cry. "This isn't good. He was so mad at me, and now. . ."

"Did you have a fight, Genevieve?"

"We did," I cry. "Over Ty."

"Who is Ty, is he there?"

Her question takes a moment to sink in.

Why is she asking me about Ty?

"No. He's my ex, he doesn't matter. Please wake my husband up." My breath shortens as my periphery grows dark and blurry. "Oh god, I can't breathe. This isn't happening. This can't be real."

"Genevieve, did you and your husband have a fight?"

"More like a disagreement, it happens sometimes after sex." I start to hyperventilate.

"Genevieve, listen to my voice. Can you hear me?"

"Yes." My voice, barely above a whisper.

"We're going to try some breathing together, okay?"

I nod in response.

"Genevieve, are you still there?"

"I'm here." I wheeze.

"Let's take a deep breath in for four. One, two, three, four."

I breathe as instructed.

"Hold it for four, three, two, one. And exhale. One, two, three, four. Now do it again."

I obey as if on autopilot. Still, it works. My heart rate slows and my breathing returns to normal. My limbs don't feel quite so heavy.

"That's good, Genevieve. Good. Do you want to tell me what happened?"

"I don't know what happened. I went to sleep last night and now—" I hear footsteps rush at me from behind. A hand grips my upper arm and pulls me to the side as paramedics surround Harrison's body.

"Are you Genevieve?" a voice asks.

"I am." I keep waiting for Harrison to wake up and prove this was all a big mistake so everything can just go back to normal.

A female officer blocks my view of what's happening. "Would you like to tell me what happened?"

I try to look over her shoulder, to see what going on. The sight of them picking his body out of the water to lay on a stretcher beside the pool makes me shiver.

"Can we get a blanket over here?" she calls out; moments later I'm surrounded by a musty smelling gray blanket. It's scratchy, but it's warm.

"I don't know what happened," I tell her.

"Why don't we go sit down over here." She motions to one of the lounge chairs on the other side of the pool. Even further away from where Harrison's lifeless body lingers. My feet don't want to move, and it takes the officer forcibly guiding me, one hand at my lower back, to get them to cooperate.

Nothing seems to be working for the paramedics either. I raise a shaky hand to my mouth. It smells like chlorine.

"Genevieve, can you tell me what happened?" She takes the phone from me—I didn't even realize I still had it—and mumbles something to the 9-1-1 dispatcher before disconnecting the call.

"I can't. I don't remember anything after we went to bed."

"Why don't you tell me the last thing you do remember," she urges.

"This morning. I came to look for him and saw him floating in the pool. He wasn't breathing."

"What time was that?"

"I'm not sure. Maybe twenty or twenty-five minutes ago."

"Why were you looking for him?"

I can't stop looking at the people surrounding Harrison. He's clearly not waking up and it appears nothing they try to revive him works.

"Uh." I look back at the officer. "He didn't make the coffee."

"Does he usually make coffee?"

"Yes."

"Were you upset that he didn't?"

"No. Just confused. It was unusual. He's always up early to make the coffee and leaves me a mug by the bed. He doesn't sleep much, but he's okay with that. Was okay with it."

"Why do you say that?"

"Obviously, he's dead." I gesture to the body they've stopped trying to revive.

"We're just going to have to wait and see what the

medical examiner says, and then we'll go from there." She rubs my back in an awkward motion, as though any type of touch will be reassuring at this point.

"He's not waking up. . ." The words drift from across the pool.

"No!" I scream, I want to rush to him but my legs give out and I sink to the ground, my chin falling to my chest, too heavy to continue holding up. "This can't be happening. It can't be. This isn't real." I rock back and forth, clutching the blanket to me, willing the words I chant to come true. Someone starts to scream. I cover my ears to drown out the noise before I realize it's me. The female officer kneels before me, her mouth is moving but the words jumble in the space between us.

I can't make them out.

The only thing I hear are the sounds of my own cries echoing in the air.

4

Genevieve

The medical examiner arrives and officially declares Harrison dead. The police continue to try to help me figure out what happened. I have no idea what to tell them. It's as though they think asking the same questions over and over will somehow make an answer materialize. It takes the female officer finally asking something that makes sense to jog my memory again.

"Why do you think you didn't wake up last night, Genevieve?"

"My sleeping pills." I decide to lead with the truth. "I take them, usually with wine, it's the only way I sleep," I begin. "After I took one last night, I went to sleep. Everything else is blank." I shake my head. "I wish I could help more."

"Maybe more will come to you if we get you away from here." The female officer gestures to where Harrison's body remains, now covered by a sheet. "We can help you get it all sorted out while our colleagues handle this here. A change of scenery would probably do you good."

I nod and let the office guide me out of the pool area, back through the gardens, to the front of the house, and into the back of the police car.

I watch the familiar scenery pass me by. Our driveway. The street we live on. The small-town center just beyond our neighborhood. The edge of town. Somewhere along the way, I realize what is happening.

"Wait, this is a mistake," I start, knocking on the cage separating me from the officers in the front seat. "I shouldn't be here. I didn't do anything. Am I under arrest?"

"You are not under arrest, Mrs. Daniels. We just thought you might benefit from talking to us on neutral ground, somewhere quiet."

"But we're at the police station." I point out, unnecessarily as we pull into the parking lot. "That's not neutral. Do I need to call my lawyer?"

"Do you think you need to call your lawyer?" the female officer asks as she assists me in exiting the back of the car.

"If you think I killed my husband, I do."

"No one is saying that," the other officer replies.

"Then it shouldn't matter if I call him," I say. "Wait, I don't have my phone with me, can you take me back so I can get it?"

"We have one you can use," the other officer says.

They usher me into a small room with a table, four chairs, and a phone. "Dial '9' to get an outside line," the officer says before shutting the door.

I dial the number I know by heart, thanks to being Harrison's assistant for so long. He often has dealings with his attorney. And his attorney is the only attorney I know.

"Grant Show," he answers.

"Grant, hi, it's Genevieve—"

"Where the hell is he? I've been waiting for almost an hour. He's not answering his phone, you're not answering your phone. Where are you calling from?"

"The police station," I whisper even though no one is in the room with me.

"What did he do?" Grant asks.

"Nothing. He's dead. And I think they think I did it. Can you come?"

"Fuck. I'm not a criminal defense attorney, Genevieve. I can't help you."

"The officer said I'm not under arrest. I just need a friendly face with me right now. Please?"

He sighs heavily. "Say nothing, I'll be right there."

I feel completely alone sitting here, even knowing all the while I'm being watched. I know enough to know I'm in a bit trouble. My husband is dead. The police are looking at me as the prime suspect. And I admit, if I didn't know me, I'd suspect me, too.

If I didn't do it, and I must believe I didn't—despite the blank in my memory—I need to figure out who would want Harrison dead.

My chest tightens uncomfortably. I don't even have anyone I can call. Anyone who might talk to me I know through Harrison. I lost touch with all my Seaside friends after moving to Lake Oswego. And our lives in Lake Oswego revolve primarily around Harrison, socially and otherwise.

Regardless, I go through the short list in my head of people I can reach out to. Half I already know won't even pick up, having been Harrison's friends more than mine. I need an ally. Someone outside of his sphere.

My head throbs and stomach churns. I need a shower to

clear my mind. And get rid of this chlorine smell. Why is it so strong?

And something, anything, to make this bad taste leave my mouth. Though I fear that may never happen now.

THIRTY MINUTES LATER

The officers don't return to the room they've stashed me in until they have Grant in tow.

He hands me a cup of coffee. "Just so we are all clear. I'm not a criminal defense attorney. There is no attorney-client confidentiality privilege. I am a friend of the family." He takes a seat next to me, leans in and whispers, "Have you said anything?"

I shake my head in response.

"Is this an interrogation?" he asks the officers.

"No," the female officer says. "We just want to ask her a few questions."

"I'd like a minute alone with her first," he responds.

The officers step out and Grant turns to me. "Did you do it? Wait, don't answer that. What the hell happened?"

"I don't know." Tears start to slip down my face. "I woke up this morning, and he was dead in the pool. I called 9-1-1, and now we're here."

"Anything happen last night?" he asks.

"Nothing out of the ordinary."

"Where's your passport?" He frowns as writes a few things down.

"The house. In the safe." I rub my eyes; I can't recall the last time I've cried so much or so hard.

He continues talking, seemingly oblivious to my state of mind. "You may have to surrender it if this goes any further.

I'm sure the accounts will be frozen. I hope you have access to cash because you're going to need it to secure the lawyer and a good private investigator. I can recommend some defense attorneys." He lays his pen down on his notepad and looks at me.

"Why?" I ask.

He sighs. "Genevieve, they didn't bring you down here to ask a few questions, despite what they say. They brought you down here so they can arrest you as soon as you say something incriminating."

"But I didn't do anything."

At least, I don't think I did.

"When has that ever stopped them?"

"Why can't you help me?"

"I'm not a criminal defense attorney. And you aren't technically under arrest. But . . ."

"It doesn't look good, huh?"

Grant shakes his head. "Not even a little. If it makes you feel better, I know you adored Harrison and I have never known you to be violent. I've even seen you save a spider. Do you remember that time you coaxed it into a cup and then brought it outside instead of letting Harrison just step on it?"

What an odd thing for him to remember. And bring up. I blink. "Thank you. I think."

He nods before slipping me a pill from across the table. I swallow it down with the coffee and smile, grateful for whatever it is, not bothering to ask.

"Xanax in case you're wondering," he mutters.

"I'm not." I don't care what it is if it numbs my mind and fills the emptiness I feel inside.

Grant moves to open the door for the officers, "Alright,

let's get this over with." He waves an arm in the air as if to say, go ahead, and takes a seat next to me.

The other officer is the first to talk this time. "Why don't you start from the beginning and tell us what happened."

"I woke up this morning—"

"It looks like you mentioned earlier there had been a fight last night. Can you start there?" The female officer interjects.

"I did?" I don't remember admitting that.

"I have the transcript from the 9-1-1 call right here." The female officer holds up a sheet of paper.

"Uh, sure." I collect my thoughts to begin again. "We had a little disagreement before bed—"

"About . . ." The female officer looks at her notepad. "Ty, right?"

"What? No." I look back and forth between the questioning faces before me.

"No?" she questions.

"Well, yes. Not a disagreement really."

"What would you call it?"

"More like a discussion?" It comes out sounding more like a question than I'd like.

"You told the 9-1-1 operator that it was a fight. Which is it?"

I'm shocked that I told the 9-1-1 operator that. It's not usually something I talk about. Ever. Our fights about Ty fall into the proverbial file of things that are never mentioned in order for Harrison and me to put forth the ideal that we have a perfect marriage. It's just not something we typically talk about. Or, rather, talked about. Everyone we know thinks we have . . . had. . . the perfect marriage. Even our marriage counselor didn't know about Ty. Harrison forbade it. So, I try to sell the lie instead.

"I must have been in shock. And not my right mind. Talking crazy." I laugh uncomfortably and twist my finger next to the side of my head as indication of such. "We were debating over where to vacation next."

"Debating?"

"Yes. Maldives versus a South American rainforest."

After I say that, I'm not sure why. Lying to the police is stupid, obviously. But I'm so used to lying about Ty's role in my marriage—or lack thereof—that it's second nature now. An automatic reflex. Something I wouldn't know how to stop if I could. Now that it's out there, all I can do is stick with it.

"And which were you? Maldives or?"

I clear my throat. "Maldives. Harrison wants, er, wanted, to trek through nature, camping and what not. And my idea of camping is no room service." I chuckle, to show I'm kidding, but I sound awkward, I can hear it.

"Would you say you're accustomed to a pampered lifestyle, Mrs. Daniels?"

"No, I wouldn't say that exactly. I was joking. Exaggerating a bit. I do that when I'm nervous."

"Why are you nervous, Genevieve? May I call you Genevieve?"

"Are you kidding?" I gesture around the table. "I'm here in a police station being questioned about my husband's death which just happened mere hours ago." I don't answer her question about my first name.

"My apologies. Let's stick to the facts and not exaggeration. That will help all of us in the long run."

"Of course." I feel slightly chastised, which is annoying. "Harrison was upset and decided to go for a swim before bed."

"And what did you do?"

"I went to bed."

"Just like that?"

"Yes."

"And you didn't worry when he didn't return right away?"

"I was asleep."

"Are you usually a heavy sleeper?"

"No, I'm a terrible sleeper. I take pills to help me sleep."

"We noticed an empty wine bottle in the kitchen and a glass on the side of the bed. Did you have wine with your pills?"

I look to Grant before saying anything; even though I'm pretty sure this has already been asked and answered. He nods.

"Yes," I say. "It helps them to work better."

"How much wine did you have?"

"I don't know. A couple of glasses maybe. Over the course of the night."

"Are you aware that you aren't supposed to mix alcohol with sleeping pills?"

"Yes."

"Do you make a habit of ignoring warning labels?"

"Excuse me?"

"It is common knowledge not to mix medication and alcohol."

"Or anti-depressants," the other officer says. "Aren't you on Paroxetine for depression?" He holds up his cell phone, showing a picture of the various pill bottles in my medicine cabinet at home.

"Yes." Not sure where this is going.

"So, you're in the habit of mixing a variety of pills and alcohol."

"Not when you put it like that."

"So, you don't drink wine while taking anti-depressants?"

"No, I do."

"What's the point of this, Officer?" Grant asks.

"Did you drug your husband, Mrs. Daniels?"

"God, no."

"Is she a suspect, and I missed it somehow?" Grant asks.

"No. Apologies." The officer gestures toward me. "Please continue"

I omit anything more about pills with wine and relay the remainder of the time leading up to the police arriving at the house this morning.

"That's quite a story," the female officer says.

I wipe tears from my face.

"I take it we're through?" Grant asks.

The two officers look at each other and stand. "Okay, Mrs. Daniels," the other officer says. "Thank you for your time. I assume we can reach out with any additional questions?"

"Of course." I nod.

Grant stands. "Give me a second, and we'll get you out of here," he says before disappearing behind them.

He leaves me alone in the room with nothing but my thoughts for company—never a good idea. I spend a lot of money on wine and pills to *not* ever be alone with my thoughts. The Xanax Grant gave me is barely making a dent in the oppressive wall of emotion currently weighing me down.

The door opens and Grant pops his head in. "We can leave. You just need to stay reachable."

I nod. "Anything to find the killer."

His head tilts. "You do realize that you can't stay at the house, right? It's a crime scene now. The police will let you collect some things. You'll be escorted and watched, naturally."

"Where am I supposed to go?" My heart pounds. I hadn't considered this. "I didn't know. I didn't think…"

He waves a hand like he wants to silence me, or maybe he simply doesn't care. "Do you have somewhere else to go without leaving the state?" he asks stressing the last part. I'm guessing to reinforce I can't go to our home in Washington.

"I can go to the Seaside house, I guess," I say.

"I'll take you there after we grab some of your things."

"I can drive myself," I protest.

"They aren't going to let you take your car, Genevieve. The entire house is a crime scene. When I say they'll let you take a couple of personal items under supervision, I mean it."

"Okay." I follow him down the hall toward the exit.

Grant moves to stand beside me in what I hope is a show of support. I need all of it I can get right now. I have a feeling my life as I know it is over. And why wouldn't it be. My husband is dead and I'm the prime suspect.

5
____

Genevieve

Grant parks up in front of our house in Seaside, Oregon. Harrison knew how much I love the ocean —how much I love the sound of the waves crashing on the shore. When this property came up, he bought it without a second thought. It's been my favorite place to be ever since.

"Do you want to come in?" I ask Grant, not really meaning it, but also not wanting to be alone. It feels like the polite thing to do after he drove over ninety minutes to bring me here.

"No," he says. "I suggest you check around for any cash Harrison may have stashed away. Unless you have accounts of your own that don't include him. The joint accounts will be frozen, but yours will be okay until you're charged."

"Until?"

"Unless." He runs his palm down his face. "I meant unless."

I nod, not sure my voice is working.

"I'll email you a list of criminal defense attorneys I recommend. Call one. Soon."

I nod again.

I stop at the door and turn to Grant. "I didn't do it. You must believe me."

"Genevieve, just call one of the numbers I send, okay?" He rubs my arms, which gives me no reassurance at all.

What makes me think I'm innocent when my own attorney thinks I'm guilty?

Grant's face softens. "Stay here, keep a low profile, don't do anything that might make you look guilty. Go about your normal day. Just make it a normal day where you're grieving your dead husband. Yeah?"

I don't respond. I no longer have the energy to talk to him. It's obvious he doesn't believe I'm innocent and that's just annoying me now.

I shut the door and lock it before either of us says anything else.

I wait until I hear his car leave the drive before stepping away from the front door to survey the empty house.

A cleaning service comes once a week to clean and stock the fridge. Before now I would always complain it was such a waste to have food sit for a week before throwing it away. But now that I'm here, in the situation I am, I'm grateful for the waste.

It's funny how things change.

I grab a bottle from wine cabinet to open, and bring it, along with a glass, to the master bedroom. Sitting on the floor, I lean my back against the wall and stare out at my favorite view from the house. The sun will start to set soon, but for the now it still glints off the water making the entire ocean appear like glass.

I pick up my phone to call his daughters. I'm sure they've been notified by now and I want to make sure they are okay.

That's dumb, they aren't going to be okay.

At the very least, I want them to know we're in this together.

Thinking of his daughters makes me think of Harrison.

I think of the last time we were in this cottage together. Valentine's Day, he brought me here for a surprise weekend. He said no phones, no business, just me and him in front of the fireplace cuddled up with a glass of wine. That's when he told me the first day he'd met me, he knew I was going to be the love of his life.

And it made me smile. Memories like that will haunt me if I find out I did kill Harrison.

Memories like that may haunt me, anyway.

My sleeping tablets can't be so strong, they make me forget everything, can they?

Isn't that why you mix them with wine?

I shake my head trying to clear my thoughts, if I keep thinking this way, I'll convince myself I did it. And the moment I do, I may as well plan on spending the rest of my life in prison for a crime I may not have committed. I decide to wait until tomorrow to call Harrison's twin daughters, Eerie and Curious, they are bound to be devastated.

I pour myself another glass of wine, the bottle now half gone. Why do I even bother with a glass?

I wonder if they have wine in prison, then laugh at my own sordid thought.

No matter how many issues we had in our marriage, deep down I know I didn't kill Harrison. I couldn't.

I know I need help, that I can't do this alone. I don't know who I can call to help me

Yes, you do.

There's only one name that comes to mind. The only person in my life who might believe that I'm innocent. Problem is, it's been four years since we've talked. I may talk *about* him a lot, but I haven't talked *to* him. If I'm honest, I'm not sure if I want to call him because as of ten hours ago, I'm no longer married. Or because I truly think he can help me. Even if I did reach him, he could be married now. He could be overseas. He could hate me.

I hate me.

I finish the bottle before reaching for the phone and dialing his number. The one I'll never forget.

"Leave a message."

His gruff voice reaches through the phone and grabs at my heart, squeezing so hard I can't breathe.

I don't do what he says.

I don't leave a message.

I just hang up instead.

6

____

Tyler

I 'm slow to wake after my night of bottles named Jack and Jim and two ladies named . . . well fuck, I don't remember their names. Doesn't matter. Didn't fuck 'em. Whiskey dick set in before I had a chance to. Right in the middle of the brunette's blowjob. Nothing like a limp dick to make you feel like a man.

Crack open the free bottle of water from the dresser and pop on the news.

"If you are just tuning in, our top news story for the day: World renowned thriller writer Harrison Daniels has been murdered. Police have yet to identify a suspect in the crime. His body was discovered earlier yesterday by his wife Genevieve Bujold Daniels. The body appeared to have been dead and floating in the author's pool for some time before she found him and called the authorities. No word yet on whether Genevieve Daniels is a suspect in the crime. As you may remember Sarah Smythe Daniels, Harrison's ex-wife, recently released a scandalous tell-all memoir about her life with the famed writer and

raising his twin girls Eerie and Curious Daniels. Harrison's camp claimed the content was libelous and threatened legal action if the publisher did not recant several of the stories. To our knowledge here at KNSS news, nothing had been filed with the courts at the time of Harrison Daniel's death. KNSS news has also not been able to reach Sarah Smythe Daniels for comment. We will continue to keep you updated on this developing story as more news comes available."

I tune the newscasters out, sinking to the bed, head hanging between my knees.

What the fuck is going on?

I grab my phone out of habit. Ready to call who the fuck knows.

There's a missed call notice blinking on the screen.

Seaside number.

Doesn't take a rocket scientist to figure out who the fuck that was.

She's got to be at their Seaside house if he was killed in Lake Oswego.

Fuck my life.

I text Al asking for the address. She has it back to me in a matter of minutes. I jump on my bike and head out.

The hard part, I realize as I'm sitting at a light waiting for it to change, is going to be coming face to face with her for the first time in four years. When you hate someone as much as you love them—it's a frustrating feeling—last four years of my life have been filled with both for this chick. I knew she'd be pissed that last time I spun up again. I never figured she'd move out.

That was my mistake.

Hers was never lettin' me explain.

If you don't consider she up and disappeared, marrying that douche bag, then leaving Seaside without a word. If she hadn't married a pseudo celebrity, I'm not sure I would've found her.

I'm sure Al could've.

The light changes and I rev my bike taking the turn onto Sunset Boulevard way faster than I should. My nerves are already frazzled, and I haven't even seen her yet. Gotta be the worst idea I've ever had.

I could've had Al dig deep when I returned from overseas to find her, but I didn't. Instead, I soothed my wounds with alcohol and women. Including Al. A mistake that almost tanked my working relationship with Mack, given Al is best friends with Daria, Mack's girl. I drive right past her house, lost in my thoughts. Turn around and cruise back, cut the engine and coast down the drive. There aren't any other cars around, and the blinds are shut, but I know she's here. I can feel it.

Still, I hesitate.

What are you afraid of?

I find my balls and head to the front door.

7

———

Genevieve

I didn't sleep well last night, despite two sleeping pills and a bottle of wine. It's not anything new that I didn't sleep, but the reasons are different. Images of Harrison's body kept invading my dreams. The blood. Bulging eyes. Bloated body. It was him and not him at the same time. It's like I'm locked inside one of his novels.

My head pounds as if someone is knocking on it.

I rub at my eyes, trying to wake. The pounding continues.

Is that the door?

The ringing of the bell answers my question for me. I peek out the window, fearing fans or the press, but see nothing. The driveway looks bare.

Pounding. Ringing. It's incessant.

It must be Grant.

I rush to the door and open it. Not bothering to glance in the mirror to see what I'm wearing or what I look like.

Doesn't matter.

Nothing could have prepared me for what awaits me when I open the door nor the question that follows.

"Why the fuck did you call me?"

8

***

Tyler

I look at her, waiting for an answer. She's a wreck. Looks about as good as I feel, which is shit.

"Ty?" Genevieve blinks rapidly. "Is that you?" Her hair's a mess of curls and tangles, eyes bloodshot and puffy, face splotchy like she's been crying. Which I'm sure she has. Still, my eyes travel her scantily clad body with a mind of their own. Nipples I remember well, protruding through the thin tank begging for attention. Skimpy boy shorts resting on narrow hips that used to be generous and grabbable, followed by thighs now way too skinny.

What the fuck has she done to herself?

"Yeah, it's me," I answer drily.

"How did . . . what?" She looks confused, head cocked, eyes squinting.

"You called me last night. Why?"

She scratches at her head. "I didn't leave a message."

"Nope."

"It wasn't my phone."

"Nope."

"How'd you know it was me?"

I push past her into the house, no longer satisfied standing on the front stoop while she gets her shit together. Door wide open for all the world to see her half naked in her fucking panties.

"Coffee?" I ask, my tone brusquer than I intend, but it doesn't bother me.

"No." She shakes her head. "I mean, yes, but not made."

"Come in," she adds unnecessarily after I'm locking the door behind me. "I'll put a pot on."

"Get dressed first," I say, gesturing to her lack of clothing.

"Oh!" She looks down at herself, like she's surprised. "Oh, god, I'll be back."

She leaves the room and I take the time to survey the house. About what I'd expect, huge windows with non-stop water views, lush leather furniture, wood floors, granite counters, crystal chandeliers. Bunch of shit that's unnecessary and fancy. Crap no one buys for their own enjoyment but for how it looks when others visit.

"Sorry about that," she says returning, having put on stretchy pants and a matching jacket, hair now pulled up with some kind of bootie or slipper on her feet.

I take a seat on a stool at the kitchen island and watch her move around the room. The feel of it all way too domesticated already.

"So?" I ask, impatient for an answer to my earlier question.

"Yeah," she says. "Wow. How are you?"

"Cut the shit, Genevieve. What the fuck is going on? Did you kill your husband?"

She blinks back at me, eyes watering. "Do you really think that? You of all people?"

"After what you did to me, pretty sure you're capable of anything, darlin'."

"What I did to *you*? What about what you did to *me*!" she cries.

"I went to find my brother's killer!" My voice rises, emotions already too tense for this. Never should've fucking come here. "Look, no one knows better than me how quickly your feelings can change."

"My feelings didn't change." She sighs. "You know what, it doesn't matter. I called you because I thought you might be an ally. My only ally really. But I see now I was wrong."

"Why the fuck would I be your ally? Of all the people you know? After what you did?"

"What did I do except live my life after you chose work over me. Again."

"My brother had just died. I was devastated." I'm admitting too much. I need to cut this short now before I say something I'll regret. "Clearly we aren't getting anywhere with this." I take a deep breath and soften my voice. "What makes you think I can help you? Or be an ally?"

The coffee maker beeps it's finished; she rises to get mugs and fill them before returning to the island. "Well, first I guess I thought you'd believe I was innocent." She takes a sip. Her pink tongue peeking out to taste the edge of the mug before closing her lips around it. A habit I'd forgotten about until just now. A move that goes right to my dick. He jumps in response, remembering her tongue well.

I shift in my seat. "I don't even know what happened."

She laughs, sardonically. "Yeah, me neither."

"Start from the beginning. The day before." I tell myself I want to know it all for the purpose of helping her. But part of me hopes she'll admit their marriage was shit. And if she did kill him, there was a good reason for it.

"We had a nice evening together, then we . . . um, let's just say we started discussing where to go for vacation." She stops and wipes the tears away from her cheek. "A trip for the two of us. He wanted to go trekking through some jungle in Costa Rica. I wanted to go to a resort by the water in Maldives. It wasn't a fight, it was just a little argument. A disagreement." She shakes her head a little. "It went back and forth for a while, he had his reasons, I had mine. It was normal couple stuff." She sighs and shakes her head.

I can't believe what I'm hearing. "You fought over where to vacation?" I scoff.

"I know it seems trivial. But we got along so well, there were hardly ever things to disagree about."

I roll my eyes. "What happened after that?" Because so far this sounds like a load of shit if she's being real with me.

"Nothing. He didn't want to go to sleep yet, so he went for a swim. I took a sleeping pill and went to bed. When I woke the next morning I found him floating in the pool, and he was already dead."

"If I get a copy of the police report, is it going to say the same thing?"

"Of course it is. I didn't kill Harrison though; you have to believe me."

Everything she's just said bounces around in my brain. Something doesn't add up. The fight doesn't sound serious. They were planning a vacation. Whole thing wrapped up in a bow.

"What is your attorney saying?" I ask.

She lets out a hollow laugh. "Nothing. I had Grant come to the station. He's the attorney for the business and works for Harrison." Genevieve groans. "Worked for Harrison. He...he's the only attorney I know." She pushes her empty coffee mug away. "He said I need to get a criminal defense attorney." She looks down at her hands wringing them together. I'm not surprised he said that to her, by all appearances everything is pointing to her.

"Why would someone think you're guilty?" I ask.

"I don't know."

"Really?"

She shrugs.

"No crazy fights in public? No marriage counseling? Fucking on a regular basis?"

She looks down at her coffee, blushing.

"We went to counseling. Who doesn't?"

I don't answer that. Plenty of couples don't.

"We were trying for a baby," she says softly.

My gut tightens, a wave of nausea washes over me. I asked the question, but I'm not ready for the answer.

She was supposed to have my babies. Not his.

Let it go, Ty. That was another life.

"So, yes on the fucking," I say.

She nods.

"Was it good?"

Silence.

"What's the matter? Cat got your tongue?"

Silence still.

"Was. It. Good?" I repeat.

She shakes her head.

"He couldn't get it up?"

"No, he could."

"Couldn't keep it up." I snicker. "If I remember correctly, you need it up and you need it hard. Ain't that right, Genie?"

"It was fine."

"Fine? *Fine?* Fucking should never be *fine.* Who the hell are you, Genevieve?"

"Harrison and I were—"

"Were what?"

"We were not sexually compatible."

"What the fuck does that mean?"

"The sexual attraction in our relationship was one-sided."

"Whose?" My voice is rough. I don't like that I need confirmation on the answer.

"His." Her chin drops to her chest, cheeks burning.

"Did you cheat on him?"

"Of course not. I would never hurt him in that way."

"But you could lay there like a dead fish when he fucked you?"

"It wasn't like that," she protests.

"How was it, Genevieve?" I can't help but ask.

"He just enjoyed it more than I did."

I sit back in my chair, cross my arms over my chest, and let the smug as fuck feeling shine through on my face. "Couldn't make you come."

She doesn't respond. Just continues looking at her coffee like it holds all the answers to life's questions.

"Any reason anyone would want to kill him?"

"No, everyone loved him."

I cock my head at that answer. She ignores it.

"Why call me?" I frown. She told me what happened that night, and she told me she didn't do it, but not once has she revealed why she reached out to me at all.

"I want you to help prove I didn't do it. I know I have no right to ask you after I left the way I did—"

"Genevieve, you deserted me."

"I didn't feel like I had a choice. You were spinning up again, wouldn't tell me why—" She stops mid-sentence biting her bottom lip in a way that makes me think about her mouth on my dick.

"There were things going on I couldn't tell you. You know that."

"There were always things going on you couldn't tell me."

"That's how security clearance works, babe."

"You should have trusted me!"

"That's not how it works either!"

"You promised you wouldn't leave."

"I didn't have a choice."

"You always—" She flings a hand in the air dismissing me. "You know what, let's leave the past in the past for now. Obviously, we can't agree on—forget it. Will you help me or not?"

There's something she's not sharing. Whether it's about leaving me, or her husband dying I'm not sure.

But I'm going to find out.

9

———————

Genevieve

He hasn't really said a word since I've told him what happened. Or at least the version of what happened that I plan to admit to.

I just can't tell if he's trying to work out whether to help me or not?

We've been sitting her now for almost five minutes, not saying anything. I know it got a little heated, but I didn't expect him to just shut down.

I study him. It's not like I forgot how ruggedly beautiful he is. But having him here, this close to me, is intoxicating. Like the reminder I never needed. I'm not sure I can handle him being around. But I know for certain I don't want him to leave. Even if that would probably be for the best.

"I shouldn't have called. I'm sorry." I stand to show him out, but Tyler stops me with a wave of his hand.

"I believe you." He meets my gaze and holds it. For the first time since this started, I feel relief. No one else . . . not

Grant, not the police at the station, not the neighbor I saw as I watched the sunset last night, has seemed to believe me.

"You need a criminal defense attorney?"

I sigh. "I know. Grant said he'd send me a list of five lawyers he recommended. I need to go through them to see if one will take my case." I look to my hands in lap and pick at my peeling nail polish.

"Don't work with an attorney referred by the attorney of the victim. I got a couple guys. Defense attorneys. Good ones. They won't hesitate to take your case. One owes me. Let me give him a call and set something up."

I don't look up. I can't yet. I'm not ready for the look on his face, whatever that may be. Tyler leans forward and snaps his fingers in front of me so I look at him. "Pay attention. I'll find the truth." His beautiful brown eyes stare back at me, and I can see he really does believe me.

This is all I needed . . . hope.

I give him a nod, because if I speak, I might cry. Finally, I have someone who is going to help prove I didn't kill Harrison.

Tyler walks into the other room to make his call. I turn to my left to look out at the beach. For a moment, I try to zone out and only listen to the waves crashing against the shore. I need peace in my head, even if it's only temporary. Ever since I woke up and discovered Harrison's dead body, I've been living a nightmare I can't seem to emerge from. And even though I believe I'm innocent, there's always a chance I'm not.

～

"WHO WERE HIS ENEMIES? Anyone he didn't like or fought with?" Tyler has not let up with his questions. We have an appointment with his attorney friend tomorrow. Since speaking with the guy he's been peppering with new ones.

"As far as I know, everyone liked him."

"Does he have any paperwork or files, cell phone records, etcetera? Anything that might give us insight into a side of him you may not have known?"

"There is no side of him I didn't know."

"You'd be surprised," Tyler says cryptically.

We walk around the house hoping I can find Harrison's safe. I'm sure he'd told me about it, probably even the code for it. And for the life of me, I can't remember. At this point, I can't even remember what day of the week it is.

Eventually, Ty finds it in the master bedroom closet behind a picture. I walk in slowly, feeling unnerved.

What was the code?

I try his birthday. It beeps angrily, all the lights turning red.

I try my birthday. Same result.

Our wedding anniversary.

Nope.

The first day I started working for him?

Finally, the door clicks open, making me smile. He said he always wanted to remember the first day he saw me. Said it was the best day of his life, and he knew I would marry him, and it always made me laugh, because he was so sure of it.

The safe opens and I pull out all the files that are in there. I have no idea what it includes. This safe holds our personal effects. Harrison handled all of that. I figured he would be here if I needed anything.

Not anymore.

I hand it all over to Ty, leaving the safe open in case we

need anything else. Even though the rest of what's in there looks like a few pieces of jewelry and valuable trinkets.

He takes it back to the table in the kitchen and starts sorting through it. I grab a bottle of wine for me and bottle of scotch for Ty before joining him.

He looks at me surprised. "It's barely one in the afternoon, Genevieve."

I shake my head. "I don't care. If you don't want it, don't drink it."

He looks at the label and nods with satisfaction. I take a large gulp of wine, the calming effects settling in almost immediately.

He pulls out a thick envelope with a rubber band stretched around it.

"Shit, Genevieve, got to be at least a hundred grand in cash." He whistles as he flips through it.

"Oh, good. I knew he had cash stored away in case of emergency. I just didn't know where or how much. Grant said they'll freeze all the joint accounts in situations like this, so I'll need it for the attorney. I have my own money, but it's not much and I'm not sure if they'll freeze that, too."

"What's not much?" he asks.

"I think it's got around twenty-five thousand in it. Like a rainy-day fund."

"Fucking rich, people. Twenty-five grand for a rainy day. I remember when that was how much you made in a year."

"It's a figure of speech."

"You've changed," he says. I don't like his tone; it sounds too much like an accusation.

"Maybe I have."

I take my wine to the patio and leave him to deal with the paperwork on his own. I don't want to deal with what's in there right now, anyway.

I try to call Harrison's daughters but get their voicemail again. I wouldn't call us super close, but we would get together every so often for a spa day or something similar. And I was always included when Harrison got together with them. I don't want them to feel like I'm ignoring them. And that I do more for Harrison than myself.

10

———

Tyler

I study everything she found in the safe while she sits on the patio. Including an entire dossier on me documenting everything I've done over the past five plus years. Fuck if I can tell she knew about it or not. Not that it would change anything. Can't trust her. Can't not trust her. Hate this is how I'm talking to Genevieve again.

I grab my phone to make a call. I need a copy of the police report before I start going through all this. I still can't tell if the dots connect with her story. Or more to the police's story? Maybe the dots are all over the fucking place and don't meet up at all.

Already know pretty much most of the police departments everywhere in the area. I look through my contacts and ring a guy who owes me a favor. I just need an idea of what they are thinking happened. And how involved they've decided she is. You can be damn sure they've already decided one way or another.

"Hey, Tyler, what has you reaching out today?" he asks.

"Need a favor if you can."

"Let me guess. You're calling about the murder, the one involving Genevieve."

I have to laugh. Known this guy for a while. As in, since before Genevieve left me and what happened after.

"She wants me to help her," I tell him. "I don't know man."

"You need the report?"

"If you can." I know it's a huge thing to ask him, but it's the only way I can be one step ahead of this.

"Tyler, you know that's not going to be easy to do."

"I know, man, I know. If you can, I'd appreciate it. If not, no worries. I'll owe you two for this." Not that either of us ever keep track. It's the offer that counts.

"Okay, give me some time. I'll hit you up you this evening if I've got anything. And, hey, careful man. Don't let your feelings for her get in the way of the truth. If she did it, she did it. You know that right?" There it is, if anyone was going to tell me to watch my back and not be fooled, it was him.

"I know. It's why I need the report. See if it connects with what she told me."

"I'll get back to you either way tonight."

"Thanks, brother."

I call in a different favor next.

Access to the death house. I need Martin, my attorney friend, to get me access in a legal kind of way.

I already have a key to both houses from Genevieve, so it's just making sure I don't fuck anything up by visiting the murder site. And that anything I may find will be admissible.

I've reviewed everything from the stack that Genevieve gave me. Harrison refers to a safe room in a few docs. I want to see what's in it. He had that house custom built with high-tech security features throughout. From exterior cameras disguised as lights to video feeds of every room—multiple angles from cameras hidden in everyday objects—to the safe room hidden in the walls with a secret entrance from his office. As much as it pains me to admit this, the man was clearly a genius. This will be the key to finding his killer.

I go through it all one more time to make sure I didn't miss anything the first time. Genevieve comes in the room and glances at the paperwork still spread out. "Did this help?"

I smile despite myself. "Believe so, babe."

"What's all in there?" she asks.

Thankfully, my phone rings so I don't have to explain. "Martin," I greet him.

"You have access. Let me know what you find." The call ends. This is how Martin operates on a case. All business. I respect that.

"I'm heading out to the Lake Oswego house."

She gasps. "Is that safe?"

"It's a crime scene. Doesn't get much safer than that."

She nods. "Okay."

I get on my bike and head out. The police took nearly twenty hours to process the crime scene. I get it. This murder is high profile. All I's must be dotted, and all T's crossed. But it's not all a waste, because I have something the police don't have, the floor plans for the house and knowledge of the safe room.

I STALL the engine before pulling into the drive. Using the code Genevieve gave me, I open the front gate and coast the rest of the way in. Parking my bike on the side where it's not easily seen from the road. No need to bring attention to myself while here.

I grab my gun from the saddlebag just in case. Then turn to take in this monstrosity that Genevieve called home. Can't fucking believe that people live like this. Stone walkway leading to a huge glass door that opens into a giant room, cavernous almost. Stone and wood treatments throughout with the only separation being a big ass double-sided stone fireplace. I picture Genevieve curled up in front of it reading one of her romance books. It was why she took the job with Harrison in the first place as his assistant, because she loved reading and thought it would be glamorous to work for an author.

Should've stopped her back then.

I take my time casing the place, not seeing any signs of a struggle, or anything that would show she was lying. At least not obvious things. Wanting to get a feel for the house before finding the safe room.

It's way too big for two people. Even if one of them had an ego as big as Harrison's. Various poster sized photos decorate one of the walls—all of Harrison with other famous people—and barely any of him and Genevieve. His office is even worse. Stark white walls covered in various self-aggrandizing pictorial tokens. Everything from blown up book covers, to best seller lists. Looks like if he could blow it up to an obnoxious size and hang it on his wall, he did it.

Finally find a picture of Genevieve on his desk. The two of them, on their wedding day. She's smiling big, with her arms around his neck, but her eyes are dead inside. Barely recognize that girl. Makes me equal parts happy combined with depressed as fuck. And Harrison? Dick looks like the spider that just caught the fly. I turn it face down out of spite and continue my self-guided tour.

The master bedroom takes up most of the second floor. Between the sleeping area, sitting area, and his and hers bathrooms and walk-in closets. The bedding is rumpled, but clearly only slept in on one side. The side closest to the door. What an asshole. Sexist as it may sound, the man sleeps closest to the door to fend off intruders. Same way he walks closest to the curb on the sidewalk. Only pussies don't put themselves in harm's way first.

Though, what if he did and that's why he's dead?

What if someone is after Genevieve?

I toy with calling her to see how she is but hold back. No one wants to kill Genevieve.

Her closet is the size of my apartment. With a crystal chandelier hanging from the ceiling and a blue suede sitting couch smack in the middle. Can't help feeling bitter about that. Little foster girl done herself good marrying up like this. I never could've provided anything comparable.

It smells like her in here, only wealthier. I sit on the couch and take it all in. Rows upon rows of silk and cashmere clothing, high-heeled shoes that've barely been worn, and purses of every shape and size. No polyester blends here. Chuckle to myself at that. She always did romanticize the glamorous life. Even when she was pretending that anything I could give her was enough. Never would have been like this. Means it never would've been enough.

My thoughts start to piss me off, so I quit wasting time and head back to Harrison's office, hell bent on finding the access point to the fucking safe room. The only thing I've needed so far that he didn't include in the safe paperwork.

I spend time studying every book, statue, painting, picture, and nick-nack. Looking for anything that seems *just* off enough. It's obvious once I find it. *In Search of Time* by some guy named Proust. Probably famous, probably something Genie's read. Don't give a fuck. Just glad that when I pull on it, one section of the bookcase swings open revealing a flat steel door behind. One with only a keypad to open it.

Bingo, motherfucker.

I enter the code that Harrison so graciously provided. The door clicks open to a room filled with monitors and machines that hum. Every monitor seems to cover a different room in the house in real time. Including the master bedroom.

I know just enough about these systems to find the index of files. A fourteen-day rotation before they're overwritten. The files are password protected when I try to click on them. Harrison didn't leave that anywhere in the paperwork either. I try a few simple four number combinations; nothing works. Have to get Al to take a look to see if she can crack it.

I notice a few more that have been downloaded and saved by date on the desktop. Curious, I click on one. Needs a password. I try Genevieve's birthday and it opens. What a sucker, using his wife's birthday as a password. Never mind that I too use his wife's birthday as a password as well.

Genevieve lies naked on the bed in the master bedroom.

Next.

Zero desire to watch their fucking sex tape. Close that one and open the next. Same password. Genevieve naked on the bed again. This time she's got a vibrator in one hand and a dildo in the other and she's using them on herself.

There's no sound.

Don't need it.

I know every one she makes when she's turned on. When she's being fucked hard. Soft. When she comes.

My dick grows restless in my jeans, I reach down to resituate, only my dick is like Pavlov's fucking dogs, sees a naked female on a bed getting herself off, must be time for him to get off too. That said, grabbing my cock feels way too good.

The fuck is wrong with me when I have to stop myself from jacking off to Peeping Tom videos of my ex-girl getting herself off in her husband's bed?

The dildo is at the entrance of her pussy and the vibrator at her clit. Her lips form an 'oh' and her eyes roll shut. I know this look. Genevieve fucks herself with the dildo, in and out, nice and slow. The vibrator circling her clit. Hips gyrating and bucking. She's giving it to herself good. I can't look away. The pink plastic of the dildo wet with her juices. She pulls it out and brings it to her mouth to lick it. Suck it. Like it's a real cock fucking her. Never have I seen such a beautiful sight as this. At least not since the last time I made her react like that.

She angles the vibrator into her entrance while rolling the dido on her tits. The words 'oh god' slipping from her lips. My cock is like steel in my jeans. Uncomfortably so.

She brings the dildo back to her pussy and sinks it in deep. I don't care how pervy it makes me. I'm about two seconds away from pulling my dick out and takin' care of business.

When I see movement in my periphery. The exterior monitor has picked up a woman walking around the outside of the house, and she's not a cop.

I look back to the Genevieve video just in time to see her orgasm.

It's exquisite.

There's no other word for it. I can do a little lip reading, thanks to my time in special forces. Which is how I know it's my name she cries out as she comes.

I close the video, feeling very aware of the fact I'm in Genevieve's house. There are quite a few other videos organized the same way. My self-control can't handle another masturbating video of Genevieve. The last one is dated the day of the murder. I click on that; it asks for a PIN like so many of the others. I try few more four number combinations and get nothin'. Grab my phone, text Al what I need her to do, along with screenshots of whatever else I think she might need.

Then quietly make my way back into Harrison's office, ready to confront the lady who just used a fucking key to get into the house.

11

Tyler

"Who the hell are you? This is a crime scene. You know you can't be here." I tell the woman wearing a skintight dress, and impossibly high heels, with her back to me.

"I'm Sarah Daniels. Harrison's ex-wife," she says lazily. As though she's got not a care in the world and is within her right to do whatever she wants. I can tell already, she's a bitch.

She turns to look at me. "I had to come and see for myself that Harrison had been murdered."

Something about her I can't put my finger on right now, but I know I don't trust her.

"Satisfied?" I ask.

She looks me up and down. "Who are you?"

"I'm investigating the case," I say telling a partial truth.

Her body tenses, she turns again so I can't read her face.

"You know she did it, right?" she offers.

"Who did what?"

"I mean, I don't want to believe it, but it seems that from everything I've heard, there isn't anyone else I could think of who had any motive." She turns to face me again, her face a mask of innocence.

"You think so?" I ask.

"I do," she says with confidence.

I know from Genevieve that Harrison had two daughters from his first marriage, twins in their teens. She had only good things to say about them. Odd, considering this is their mother.

"How are your daughters holding?" I ask, to change the subject. To my knowledge, they've not reached out to Genevieve. I can't believe they don't want to make sure she's okay and assure her of their states of mind.

"They are at home, too distraught to go anywhere." Sarah begins to walk closer to me, and I stand my ground.

"What do you think, did Genevieve do it?" she asks.

"It doesn't matter what I think."

"Well, I hope she gets put away for this. Harrison didn't deserve to die. He was a kind man, a gentle heart, he wouldn't hurt anyone, and he got this horrible death by someone he thought loved him." She shakes her head and dabs at non-existent tears.

Need to find out why Harrison split with the ex. Something about her ain't settling right.

"What I plan to prove." I follow her toward the kitchen. "Whether she did it." Then ask, because I'm curious about her take on it, "Do you know if they had any problems?"

She walks around casually, seemingly looking at nothing. "Not that I know of, but I haven't spoken to Harrison in a while. The girls spoke to him every day. They so shocked by this. That Genevieve could do such a thing."

If they think Genevieve did it, would explain why they haven't reached out to her.

Sarah turns around to face me. "Would I be able to look around?"

I shake my head. "House is still a crime scene. Shouldn't be here now."

"But you're here," she says. "And I don't see a badge."

"Got the judge's permission right here." I pull a random piece of paper from the inside pocket of my leather jacket to flash at her. She doesn't need to know I'm helping Genevieve and am only able to be here 'cause my buddy called in a favor. She stands up straight annoyed with my reply, but there is no way I'm letting her walk around the house alone. Especially now that I've found the safe room. Can't trust she won't do something with the videos or the cameras.

"And have you found anything?" She's not afraid to ask her questions. And doesn't appear to be in a rush to leave either.

"Found out Harrison had a safe room with surveillance on—" I stop when I see her body react to my words. Her shoulders tense and she starts shifting her weight from foot to foot. Doesn't look like she realizes she does it. Something on them she doesn't want me to see. "Can't get into them all just yet."

Her body relaxes. She's nervous about something on those tapes.

Is the murder on the videos? Or was it something else? Harrison having an affair with his ex?

"I'm sure there is nothing on there, except maybe proof that Genevieve is guilty. Why aren't you questioning her?"

I can't help but smile and shake my head. One of those rich people who think they can get their way easily.

"I have. Probably will again. did. Have your daughters been to talk to them yet?"

"I don't know why they would need to. They weren't at the house when it happened. Besides, they are so upset they can't talk to anyone. One mention of their dad, they start crying." She looks around the house once more. "I best get going, do you know when the house will be open for me to come?"

"Ask the police." I walk over to the door with her to make sure she leaves. Bitch is hiding something—whatever it is, I hope it's on tape.

After I'm sure she's gone, I grab my bike and head out to Martin's. Need him to figure out how we can work the safe room videos into the case legally, if at all, once Al hacks them. There's got to be proof on them, I just know it. But, I don't want to have that conversation with him over the phone.

On my way there, I call Genevieve.

"Hey," she answers, her voice soft.

"You okay?" I ask.

"I'm good."

"Just wanted to call with an update. You know Harrison had a safe room at the house with surveillance?"

"What? No! Oh god, Tyler, what if it shows I did it, I don't think—"

"Genevieve, not why I'm asking. Stay focused."

She sniffles. "Okay."

"Guessing you don't know the PIN to access the videos then?"

"No, I'm sorry."

"I'm heading to Martin's, the guy we're meeting tomorrow. Have a couple things to go over with him and I'll be back."

"Thank you, Ty. I appreciate it. You have—"

"Yep." I end the call before she starts crying over the phone and going on about how thankful she is.

12

———————

Genevieve

I decide to go through the paperwork that we pulled from the safe. I know Ty's been through it all twice and would have told me if there was anything that lead to a suspect or anything else involving his murder. But I still want to see it all for myself. Just in case. There are a few news articles about Harrison from early in his career. Funny he has them in here and not up on a wall with so many of the others. The prenup that was signed the day we got married. I never argued it, I'm the one who said I wanted to sign it. I didn't want people to think I was marrying him for his money, didn't want his daughters accusing me of anything.

Paperwork for his business holdings, which I never got involved in. Plans for the Lake Oswego house from way back when he had it built. The mortgage for the beach house, and a bunch of legal paperwork that I don't want to concern myself with just yet. Files for movie rights and options for his books, things that seem better suited for a filing cabinet than a safe. But who am I to say? As I near the bottom of the pile, one jumps out at me. I pull it from the stack and settle in to read it: a file titled Tyler Presley.

What the fuck?

Why would Harrison have a file on Ty?

And why wouldn't he tell me about it.

I leaf through it: reports, pictures, cell phone records. The reports look periodic reports, like maybe Harrison had someone checking on Tyler or following him. From before Harrison and I were even married. Each time he spun up, where he went, how long he was gone. Where he lived, how much he made, surveillance photos, pictures of Ty and I, most of which are in chronological order. How the hell did he get all this?

And then—

Oh my god!

My hands shake as they pick up the next item.

A receipt for a ring.

An engagement ring.

Ty bought me a ring before his brother died and Harrison has a copy of the receipt. Why?

And, during a time when I thought his job meant more to him than I did, he was going to propose.

And Harrison knew.

He knew Ty intended to propose the whole time he encouraged me to break it off for my own sake. And when I found out I was pregnant, it was Harrison who convinced me the right thing to do was to keep it from Ty and stay away. So my child would not have to suffer through life with their father leaving at any given time, for any length of time, with little to no contact in between.

It was Harrison who showed me statistics on the success of children raised in stable environments. Playing on my own insecurities of being raised in the foster system.

How he could provide that stability for me and the baby. Assuring me he didn't care that I was still in love with Ty. Just having the baby and I in his life would be enough for him. It makes me sick remembering how easily I bought into it all. Especially when he pointed out the importance of keeping it all from Ty, even if I could reach him, so that his focus could be on his mission and not split between there and here. For his own safety. Knowing all the while where Ty was and what he was doing. Coaxing me into marrying him, how that would solve everyone's problems.

My chest burns with the betrayal.

"Oh, Harrison."

Tears fill my eyes, only this time in anger and deceit instead of guilt and grief.

And it just gets worse from there. Tyler's undercover work, drug addiction, injury, rehab, and release from service. Honorable, but still. Pictures of the damage to his knee are devastating. The numerous surgeries, the pins and brackets that now hold it in place.

Ty was back in Seattle at about the time the baby would have been born, had she lived. By then, Harrison and I were married, and he'd whisked me off to Lake Oswego. All the while knowing Ty had returned, with me none the wiser.

How did Harrison have access to this information?

It doesn't stop there; he even has reports of what Ty has done with his new company in Seattle. Changes of address, random surveillance photos seemingly pulled from other sources. And, of course, detailed accounts of each time Ty came to Seaside. Where he went, who he talked to, and for how long. Did Harrison think Tyler would reach out to me while here? Or I him? Harrison had so little faith in me that he thought I'd cheat.

I can't wrap my head around what I'm looking at. How Harrison was able to get it, and why I didn't know about it.

Then I see the printouts of the news articles from when Ty's brother died.

Shit!

The anniversary of Ty's brother's death is today.

The impact of realizing knocks the wind from me. How could I have forgotten it was today? Something so integral to Ty's life. I'm leaning on him, asking him to help me, all the while he's going through trauma of his own.

The tears start and it's impossible to stop them. Quickly growing from silent to uncontrollable sobs. The outpour of anguish filling the silence of the room, depleting my soul, and exhausting my heart.

I cry for myself, for Ty and his brother, for Harrison and his insecurity driven betrayal, and for the baby that never was. For the life I could have led given the chance.

I cry until I have nothing at all left to give.

And then I let the darkness envelope me.

Tyler

I grab take out on my way back to the beach house. I've been running off a fast-food breakfast sandwich I had earlier, and all I want is a shower, a beer, and food.

Walking into the house, I look around to see where Genie is and find her on the patio, curled up on a bench with a blanket wrapped around her, looking out at the beach.

"I picked up some dinner," I say, as I walk over to her. Genie looks over her shoulder at me, I can't read her expression in the dark. "Mind if I grab a shower?" She returns a small nod, then looks back over at the beach without saying another word to me.

I never unpacked at the motel, so I still have the scant things I brought with me in the saddle bag on my bike. I grab my toothbrush, fresh boxers, and a clean tee before retreating into the bathroom just off the living room. The hot water on my back feels amazing after everything today. Martin and I went over the police report as well as what I found at the death house. The only thing Genie's got going for her is the lack of a murder weapon. Harrison's head had been bludgeoned, forcing him unconscious, then he drowned in the pool. Not that the official cause of death has been released, but it's obvious based on the pictures and descriptions. The question now is who had access to him late at night along with the opportunity to give him a solid knock on the head.

Genevieve.

Just can't prove or disprove it yet.

I'M NOT surprised when I see Genevieve still sitting outside on the bench when I come out of the shower. She hasn't even been for a walk on the beach, which I might get her to have one tonight.

"Do you want food?" I shout from the kitchen as I start warming up the food. She gets up and walks into the house.

"I went through all the paperwork today," she tells me, while standing on the other side of the counter.

"Yeah," I reply, putting the food on the plates.

"Found the file on you." You can hear how tired she is, she can't even get her words out, the fear she has of going to sleep is crazy. I understand the power of nightmares. How they wreck havoc on your life until you're able to get them under control.

Taking the food out to the outside table, I go back to grab a beer for me and wine for her, handing her a glass before sitting back down.

I open my beer and look out to the ocean. "You didn't know about it before?"

She shakes her head. "No."

"I find that hard to believe, Genevieve."

"Why? Apparently, Harrison kept all kinds of things from me," she says sourly. "Surveillance cameras, a safe room, an entire dossier on your life."

I nod—"Looks that way,"—and drain half my beer.

"There were so many reasons for him to tell me about that, tell me he knew where you were and what was going on."

"Like what?"

"I don't want to go into it now." She sighs. Suffice it to say, if I'd known then what I know now, maybe I would've killed him."

"Don't be tellin' too many people that." I chuckle, finishing off my first plate of food.

"Anyway, I'm sorry I forgot about the anniversary of your brother's death. Are you okay?"

That stops me for a second. Not that I forgot, but I went through the day not doing the things I normally do and I'm not sure how I feel about it. Kept my mind off it. Which can be good. But I didn't get a chance to 'talk' to my brother, which I miss.

"Don't worry about it. I'm good." I stand to grab seconds and another beer. "Need anything?" I gesture to the kitchen.

"No."

When I get back with my second plate piled high with food, I notice she's barely touched hers. But her wine glass is freshly filled. And she's turned on the outside heaters.

"You drink a lot of wine." I don't think she has a problem, at least not a serious one, I'm just curious to see what her answer is.

"Yep." She puts an unnecessary emphasis on the 'p' sound, leading me to believe she doesn't want to talk about it.

So, I change the subject. "Why'd Harrison and his first wife get a divorce?"

"He found out she was having an affair, and he couldn't forgive her for it," Genevieve tells me, which gets me thinking. Would Harrison have an affair with his ex-wife, after she did it to him?

"And how did she feel about the divorce?"

"Harrison said it was bitter, she was fighting him on a lot, but in the end, he had the better lawyer." Genevieve finishes pretending to eat her food and set's her plate aside. "Why do you ask?"

"I met her today. There was something about her which didn't sit right with me." I place my empty plate on the table and grab another beer. "Wanted to know her story," I add.

"We've never had a problem with each other. At least not much of one. She can be bitchy, throws comments around here and there sometimes about how I took him away from her, even though we all know that's not what happened. Nothing too much worse than that, though. Did she say anything about me?"

"Only that you did it."

Genevieve scoffs. "Of course. That would make her life easier. With me out of the way there'd be nothing to prevent the girls from getting everything after Harrison died." Genevieve looks at her phone. "They haven't even returned my calls." She looks up at me through her eyelashes. I can see the disappointment in her eyes. "How can I tell them I didn't do it, if they won't even speak to me?" She's about to cry.

Fuck.

I don't trust myself to touch her.

If I don't, she'll cry.

Can't fucking handle that either.

"They'll come around. Just in shock is all." Against my better judgement, I get up to go sit next to her. She leans into me like it's normal to do so. I take it one step further and wrap an arm around her. Then seal my own fate by making a promise I'm not sure I can keep. "We'll find out what happened. It'll be okay."

She wraps her arms around my waist. "Thank you for believing me when no one else does." She whispers into my chest; her body relaxes into mine.

When I lie down on that outside sofa, with Genevieve still in my arms, I tell myself it's so she can finally get some sleep without images of Harrison's floating body forcing her awake. When I start to sweat, I tell myself it's the warmth of the patio heater beating down on us, combined with a whole other body lying on me. And pretend it has nothing at all to do with my own needs or desires. And when I sleep the night through for the first time in four years, I tell myself it was the ocean air and the sounds of the waves that lulled me to it.

14

———————

Genevieve

I t's been a while since I've slept a full night on my own without the aid of pills. If it wasn't for Tyler, I don't think it would have happened. He kept me close to him all night, and I felt safe and secure.

We have a meeting with his attorney friend this morning. But I'm not ready to move from my spot yet, the same couch we woke on, an hour before. I drink my coffee, look at the beautiful blue ocean, and force myself to remember the times Harrison and I had been happy here.

Even with the weight of his betrayal hanging over me, I need to remind myself of better times. The joy in wanting to start a family. The weekends when Harrison would step away from his computer and let loose for a while. Driving up and down the coast trying to find towns we'd never been to before. Harrison making fun of me dancing in the kitchen while I cooked. How he couldn't carry a tune, but still loved to sing.

I know Tyler is doing what he can to prove I didn't do this. But when each new bit of uncovered information ends with me betrayed by Harrison, I don't always trust that I didn't. What if I found out something else he'd done, and I've pushed it to the bottom of my subconscious, then allowed myself to kill him and go back to bed as if all were normal. Ty said I'm still in shock with everything and my mind is not remembering everything it should. Anything that can help has been pushed to the back, because all I can think about is the moment I found him.

I don't know if Ty believed me when I told him I never knew there were TV monitors in the safe room, or cameras around the house. Not that I blame him. It seems pretty farfetched that I wouldn't know those things.

I know Harrison had cameras at the front door, the backyard, and any entrances coming into the house. I just didn't know there were cameras looking into every room of the house as well.

That doesn't make sense to me. By the time someone got in, we'd already have them on the outside cameras, right? I honestly thought the safe room had loads of other important paperwork that he just didn't want anyone else to get their hands on.

Makes me wonder what else was Harrison hiding from me.

I thought we were open with one another. Maybe he didn't want to tell me about the cameras because then I wouldn't be able to walk around the house so freely. Or do anything so freely. The last thing I wanted was to have sex with Harrison knowing it was being filmed.

Even thinking about the cameras around the house makes me feel weird. Part of me wonders if he put them there because he thought I'd do the same thing Sarah did to him. Cheat.

I was surprised when Tyler told me that Sarah had come to the house. Why would she be coming to a crime scene when she knows she shouldn't be there? He told me about their conversation, and the things she was saying about me, but he never told me about his meeting with Martin. He's not hiding things from me, is he? Or am I just paranoid now that I know Harrison hid so much that I think everyone is capable of it.

If he is hiding something from me, what would it be?

Stop it, Genevieve.

I remind myself things are going well with Ty. And I don't need to sabotage that by thinking he doesn't have my best interest at heart. He's done nothing to make me doubt him. Just the opposite. As crazy as it is, I've loved having Ty around. He makes me feel safe. And I don't think I've felt safe in a while.

WE DRIVE in silence for about thirty minutes, then he pulls up at his friend's house. I'd almost forgotten how good it felt to wrap my body around Ty's from the back of his bike. By the time we stop, my body is still tingling. We walk in and Tyler introduces me to the criminal defense attorney he believes will take my case.

"This is Martin. We're going to tell him everything that happened and see what he says."

I can feel him coaching me, so I nod and look at the man who could be my savior. Immediately, I'm aware of how much this matters and how much I worry I'll mess this up.

Before I speak, Martin turns to Tyler. "That's mighty

polite of you, implying I have a choice, since we both know I owe you."

My brow furrows. This is clearly some inside joke or secret. I don't expect anyone to tell me anything, but Martin looks at me and shares.

"I was about to get married. I was so in love there was no talking me into a prenup. So this guy..." He jerks his thumb toward Tyler. "...goes and checks her out behind my back without asking for a penny."

"I had a feeling." Tyler shrugs like it's no big deal. "Of course, I didn't charge you for that."

As I look around at his opulent home, I realize Martin has plenty to lose. "Tyler is a good friend," I murmur.

"Better than I deserve. I didn't even want to look at the pile of evidence stacked against her. The cheating. The drug use. The third husband who had a fatal accident. It was like I never knew her at all. I owe this man big time. Which is why we both know I'm taking the case." He stares me in the eyes. "And why do I tell you this?"

Swallowing hard, I reply, "So, I feel comfortable telling you everything."

With a nod, Martin glances at Tyler. "Smart cookie. Let's see if she's as honest." He gestures to the chair across from his desk in the study. I'm assuming we're in his office away from the office. I half expect a paralegal to pop in any minute.

"Tyler believes you're innocent, and for me, that's enough." He looks at Tyler. "Maybe most importantly, my debt to him is repaid." The men shake and I realize we have a deal.

"I'll let the district attorney know that I'm your lawyer if they decide they have enough evidence to arrest you. I know a little about your case because, obviously, it has been all over the news for the last twenty-four hours. And I reviewed the police report with Ty last night. Your husband was a well-known and wealthy man. Didn't appear to have too many people who'd want to kill him, far as I can tell. I want to hear your version of events. Tell me what they aren't reporting." He walks around his large brown desk and sits down in his leather chair.

Tyler takes a seat beside me and gives me the nod to speak.

Taking a deep breath, I tell Martin everything I had told Tyler while we were having coffee. Until we get to the fight the night before Harrison died.

What if this man really can help me?

He's already encouraged me to be honest.

What if I continue the lie I started with the police and reaffirmed with Ty?

Does it really matter what we fought about? Whether it was a vacation or Ty?

If Ty knows we fought about him, what's he going to think?

I've spent so much time lying about my relationship with Harrison, I'm not sure I even know how to tell the truth now.

What would be the harm in telling the truth? If he's my attorney, he needs to know everything. Even if it makes me look guilty.

"And what was the fight about?" Martin takes notes as I talk, writing a few things down, checking in with glances to both Tyler and me.

I close my eyes and take a deep breath, release it slowly before continuing. "It was about Ty."

I feel the man in reference tense beside me. His jaw hard, arms folded across his chest. If he's surprised, he does a good job at hiding it. But his anger radiates off him in waves. Is he mad I lied to him? Or mad I think about him?

"What about Ty?" Martin asks.

I go all in. What have I got to lose at this point? "Harrison believed I was thinking about Ty when we had sex." I look to Ty to see his reaction, but he's looking straight ahead.

"And were you?" Martin asks.

"Yes."

"Why?"

"Because that's the only way it was enjoyable. And Ty was always the man I wanted to be having sex with. Not Harrison."

Martin nods, stroking his chin as he thinks.

"May I ask why you married Harrison?"

I look to Ty. He still won't shift his gaze from what's right in front of him. His body vibrates with tension. If he's this upset over what I've just shared, he's never going to forgive me for what I'm about to. I'll be honest, a small part of me thought him showing up at my house yesterday might lead to a possible reconciliation. Not now, or anything, but maybe some time in the future. A small part, since I have no idea what's going on in his life right now. He could be living with someone for all I know. He's not wearing a ring, so I doubt he's married. I shouldn't care.

It doesn't matter, even if we had a chance, I'm about to kill it.

"Because I was pregnant."

Ty jumps up from his seat, turning to look at me, shock blanketing his face. "What?"

I look at him, my eyes pleading with him to understand. "I didn't know until after we'd broken things off and you'd spun up." Tears stream down my face. He's going to hate me, I just know it. Because this story doesn't get any better.

"Was it mine?" Ty asks.

I nod.

"Our baby? As in I got you pregnant?"

I nod again. Not sure if I can speak.

"What the fuck, Genevieve." Ty begins pacing, running his hands through his hair. I can tell he's still processing the first part of this. I'm afraid to see how he handles the second. Martin and I both remain silent until he slows to look at me again.

"You didn't tell me," Ty rasps.

"I swear. I wanted to get word to you, but I was told it would be a bad idea."

"From whom?" he demands.

"Your commanding officer for one. He said you were undercover, and it wouldn't be good to divide your focus. And Harrison agreed."

"You talked to Harrison about *my baby* before you talked to me."

"He was my friend."

Ty scoffs. "Some friend."

"And this led to you getting married?" Martin interjects. Ty resumes pacing angrily in the space behind our chairs. Any second now it's going to occur to him, there's no baby in my life right now.

"Yes. Harrison pointed out that I had no idea how long Ty would be gone and that the baby would benefit from a two-parent household. He knew that I was insecure about my own upbringing in the foster care system."

"And where is the baby now?" Martin asks softly. The question I don't want to answer. The memory breaking my heart all over again. It was the worst possible pain imaginable. I don't want to put Ty through it. No one should have to experience that.

A sob escapes my throat before I can stop it. I bring my hand up to my mouth to cover it and take a few deep breaths, trying to compose myself before I continue.

Martin hands me a box of tissue. I nod in thanks. Emotion still too heavy for me to talk. It feels like she's being ripped from my body all over again. How do I tell Ty I was carrying a baby he didn't know about? And that she died.

"She—" my voice croaks. I take a moment to blow my nose and clear my throat. I refer to the fetus as her. Because in my imagination there was a baby from the moment I learned I was pregnant. I've always wanted kids. With Ty.

"The fetus was not viable and died in the womb. We had to abort at six months. It would have been a girl." I bury my head in my hands and sob. Not caring any longer to pull myself together. It was a tragedy. I have a right to feel despair.

Ty falls to his knees, releasing something between a groan and cry of anguish. It's devasting to hear. He drops his forehead to the floor before him, rocking back and forth.

I should have known it would affect him like this, he's always wanted to be a dad. The chance to raise someone in the exact opposite way he and his brother were: with love, patience, understanding, and time.

And, I should have realized he would get angry. Ty doesn't deal with any emotion, outside of anger, well. If he starts feeling something he's not comfortable with, he just channels it to anger.

Like he's doing now.

He stands, takes a deep breath, and lets it out slowly, before approaching my chair. He leans forward, his hands resting on the arms, his face inches from mine. "Let me see if I got this straight, Genevieve," he starts. "You were pregnant with my baby and didn't tell me." The look on his face is pure hatred and anger. Even though I expected both reactions from him, I can tell now I'm not prepared for them. Any ounce of self-assurance I may have held inside me shrivels down to nothing. "Then, the baby died, and you *still didn't tell me*?" He roars the final words.

"Fetus," I whisper.

"What?"

"I'm sorry," I sob. "I thought I was doing the right thing."

"Because *he* said it was?"

I nod dumbly.

Ty cries out with rage and turns to punch the wall. Leaving a decent sized hole in his wake. Then he shocks both Martin and I by leaving. Moments later we hear his motorcycle peel out of the drive and race down the road.

My body shakes from adrenaline and fear. Not fear of something Ty will do to me, more fear of what he'll do to himself.

"So, aside from all that." Martin waves a hand at the hole Ty left in his wall. "How are you managing? Do you have everything you need?" Martin stares at me intently.

I shift in my seat, then realize what he's asking. Payment. Lawyer's like to get paid. "I'm okay financially. I have some cash Harrison left me in the safe. I can pay you for your time."

"That's not what I'm asking," Martin says, surprising me.

I look at him quizzically. "What do you mean?"

"The fortitude to get through this."

Ah, that.

"I think so."

"You feel up to telling me the rest?"

I share with him everything else that happened up until

Tyler appeared at my door yesterday morning. He takes notes on everything.

"I want to have a look at the paperwork if that's okay."

"Of course. Whatever you need." My heart is in my throat and my palms are sweaty.

"Come on." Martin stands up. "I'll give you a ride home."

15

Tyler

It's impossible to describe the anger I feel over Genevieve not telling me that she was pregnant. I had a right to know, and she took it upon herself to hold it back. But she told him. Harrison. The man I can't even hate now because he's dead but who I've spent the last four years envying thanks to the woman in his life.

I spend a few hours driving aimlessly, taking my anger out on long stretches of road and corners that are too tight for the speeds I take them at. It's reckless and stupid. I'm usually an advocate for bike safety. But tonight, I can't keep it contained.

It's not just that she was pregnant. It's the whole fucking thing. My brother dying, the breakup, the mission, my knee, rehab, time spent apart, Harrison's murder, and still not knowing if Genevieve killed him. Don't get me wrong, I don't believe she did. I don't think she has it in her. But she's changed and this new Genevieve isn't the one I know well.

Means there's always a chance I'm wrong.

And then the biggest bombshell of them all.

She thought about me when she fucked him.

And he knew it.

It's all I've thought about the last half of my ride. Makes me want to fuck her. Get it out of my system. What do I do with that?

I pull into her drive and cut the engine. I guess I'm about to find out.

I KNOCK on the front door, not wanting to just let myself in even though I still have they key from yesterday. She opens the door, relief blankets her face. "Ty, I—"

I don't let her finish. Instead, I do the dumbest thing humanly possible.

My hands grip either side of her face and before I think too long on how wise this might be, I have her backed against the wall. My mouth is on hers, my tongue pushing its way inside, a growl releasing from somewhere deep in my chest. She whimpers and wraps her arms around my neck, hanging on as I pin her to the wall with my hips. My cock already hard as steel. I don't think about the repercussions. I don't think about the future. I don't think about anything other than her, thinking about me, when she fucked him.

"Is this what you wanted?" I ask against her lips. Knowing this is a mistake on so many levels. And not fucking caring. I move my mouth to her neck and bite, hard.

She cries out. "Yes! Oh, god, yes."

I grab her legs and wrap them around my waist, opening her up to me. Her skirt gives zero resistance. I can feel the heat of her pussy even through my jeans. She gyrates against me wantonly. Pulling at my hair, my jacket, my shirt, anything she can find purchase with to pull me closer. My hands grab at her ass and my mouth makes its way to her tits. She's not wearing a bra. My mind spins, I can't think. All I can do is act. Ravenous for her skin, I rip her tank in two straight down the middle, giving me access to her luscious breasts.

She moans my name as I take one in my mouth, her nipple hardening under the assault of my tongue.

I can't get enough.

I push them together, taking both taut ends in my mouth at once, biting, sucking, slurping. Animalistic sounds emitting from my body that I barely recognize. The need to possess her so great, I can focus on nothing else.

"Missed these," I grumble.

"Please," she begs.

She pushes her hands between us to unbutton my jeans as I yank up the hem of her skirt.

My actions are frantic and jerky, like a teenage boy during his first time. It's all I can do not to come when she gets my cock in her hand.

"Oh, fuck," I moan.

I'm going to lose it. It's been too long since I've had her.

I work my hand in her panties and plunge three fingers inside her, forcing her to stretch. She's so fucking drenched. I drive them in and out of the tight space harshly as I bite at her neck. I'm not gentle. There's nothing loving about my actions. Her moans get louder and louder.

"Oh, Ty, I'm going to come!" she cries. Her eyes shut and her body clamps down around my hand. Her juices coating my fingers. I don't stop. Thrusting my fingers higher inside her. Punishing as best I can. Still angry over how things have played out. Wanting her to feel it.

"Aahhh!" she screams as she comes again in quick succession.

She's ready for me. I force her mouth back to mine and kiss her hard through her orgasm. Her breath heavy through her nose. I don't stop until I feel her muscles loosen around my fingers and her body lose its tension.

"Gonna be quick and dirty." I pull at the scrap of lace she calls panties, easily ripping them from her body. I position my cock at her entrance and slam it home.

Our twin cries meet in the space between us.

So fucking good.

It's been too long since it felt this good. I can't move. If I do, I'll come. God I've missed her.

She's so hot. Tight. Wet.

Fuck.

She's perfect.

My blood roars through my veins, drowning out the sound of her cries. I pull out slightly and look down at where we are joined. Her juices coat my cock, a sight I haven't seen in a long, long time. She tilts her hips pulling me in further, burying her face in my neck, plastering kisses everywhere she finds skin. I piston my hips, again and again, slamming inside her as hard as I can. Wanting her to feel my balls slap against her ass. I can't remember the last time I've gone at it this hard. I can feel her starting to come again, I don't even care. I fuck her ruthlessly through it as she screams in my ear. Again, and again.

The wall behind her shakes with the force of each pump of my hips. A picture falls to the ground from beside us. Probably one of Harrison's ego-boosting bullshit pictures. I'm close. So close. I wrap my hand in Genevieve's hair and pull her head back, giving me unfettered access to the sensitive skin. I can't believe how good she tastes. I bite down hard, the taste of blood tickles my tongue. She moans with satisfaction and claws at my shoulders.

I'm going to come.

I need her to get there.

One more time.

I work my hand toward her ass and push a finger in her puckered hole without preamble. Her moans grow louder.

Fuck.

I can't hold it any longer; I let go with a roar as her pussy walls clamp down on my dick again.

My muscles tighten, my knee aches, I'm blinded by the explosion of light and feeling filling my body. I stumble back, falling against the couch behind us, my ass perches on the ledge of the back. Genevieve goes limp, draped over my shoulder, breathless and sated.

I can't move.

I can't breathe.

I can barely lift my head to look at her.

I take a long moment to try and catch my breath. Only when she lifts her head do I slowly open my eyes to meet hers.

"Again," I say.

16
———

Genevieve

We stand there under the many showerheads, letting the water wash away sweat and bodily fluids. Tyler hasn't said a word since our first session against the wall. Since then, he's fucked me again on the couch, and once more in my bed. Each time more ravenously than the time before. My vagina aches from the literal pounding its taken.

He didn't use a condom.

I didn't ask him to.

And I'm not on the pill.

I'm not sure what I want to say, but when I've tried to talk, he's placed his finger against my lips to silence my voice.

He takes his time washing my body with a soft cloth and mild soap. Starting at my feet and working his way up my body. Taking care around the areas he knows are sore. Tyler is stoic and stone-like through it all. Showing zero emotion.

I don't mind. This took my mind off everything in a

fantastic and effective way. Now I reside in the post-orgasmic haze of vigorous lovemaking. Something that hasn't happened since the last time I was with Tyler over four years ago.

When he finishes washing me, I turn to tend to him. Even though I know the streams of water must hurt as they penetrate the cuts and scrapes on his bruised knuckles, he doesn't say a word. Eventually sitting on the shower bench to allow me to wash his hair. His eyes shut while my fingers run through his thick brown locks. I try to ease the obvious tension from his body, starting at the top and working my way down.

I make my way to his mid-section and further south. His hardening cock the only sign that he is alive inside. I lower to my knees and take him in my mouth, sucking first on the tip, then his entire length. When he grabs the sides of my head, I know I have him back, at least a little bit.

He takes control almost immediately. Ruthlessly fucking my face. Tears stream down my face as I gag, trying to relax my throat. I put my hands on his knees, not sure if I want to push him away or pull him closer. The decision made for me as he reaches his release with a loud groan, thick spurts shooting down my throat. I swallow as much as I can, letting the rest dribble out my mouth and wash away with the water.

I look up at him, his face a contortion of anger, regret, and something close to adoration. He pulls me to my feet, throws one of my legs over his shoulder, and feasts on me. That being the only word adequate to describe the onslaught of teeth, lips, and tongue that attach themselves to my center. It's so intense I want him to stop and at the same time keep going forever.

I orgasm quickly. Amazing considering the number of

times I've already come tonight. I try to push his head away, but he doesn't stop. Growling in return. And before I realize it, I'm coming again. And again.

Only then does he slow his onslaught, lapping gently at my folds, kissing my clit, and nuzzling my inner thighs. My body starts to come down, and I wilt against the cool shower wall. He washes me again, covering my body in small kisses between words of reverence and adoration. He turns off the shower and silently wraps me in a towel, before grabbing one for himself and briskly rubbing his body dry.

He leads me to the bed and pushes me to sit on it. Taking a second towel to dry my hair, then using the one around me to finish drying my body.

"Ty—" I start to speak, but he holds a finger against my lips to silence me once again.

He pushes me back so I'm lying toward the middle of the bed. He blankets my body with his and enters me with a single thrust. My breath leaves me with a whoosh, still sore from earlier. I prepare myself for the roughness that is soon to follow. Only this time is different.

Where I thought he would be rough and fast, he takes his time with almost lazy thrusts. Kissing me gently in all the places he bit and bruised prior. His dick moving in and out of me with a fluid and languid motion. Paired with soft touches and lingering kisses, building the pleasure to a point where I am frantic for my release.

"Ty," I moan. "Please."

He nuzzles my neck with his chin, kissing me just below my ear. A spot that makes me dizzy with desire.

When he reaches between us and pinches my clit lightly, I fall into the abyss of senseless bliss. Everything falls away except for the connection we share and the utter satisfaction it brings. He groans into his own release with one last push, so deep I feel like he'll break through me.

I don't move. I can't. Not until he rolls us over, so I'm lying on top of him. His arms tight around me, face buried in my neck. I loll against him and lay my cheek against the top of his head, trying to catch my breath. Wondering what this means—if anything.

He pulls the covers over us and settles in. It's only after I hear the first light snore, I realize he's asleep. It doesn't take me long to do the same.

17

———————

Tyler

I get up before Genevieve and head to the kitchen to make coffee, wearing nothing but my sweat bottoms. That was my first mistake.

I open the patio and step out onto it, breathing in the crisp morning air while I wait for the coffee to brew. That was my second.

Genevieve appears at the patio door wearing nothing but my T-shirt. Her hair and face have that thoroughly fucked look that makes me feel proud despite myself.

"Uh, Ty?" she calls.

I smile in return, feeling better than I have in a long fucking time. Ready to grab her and go for round five. Or would it be six?

She jerks her thumb over her shoulder.

That's when I see the police standing behind her.

"You may want to put some pants on, ma'am," one officer says.

"Genevieve Daniels, you're under arrest for the murder

of Harrison Daniels. You have the right to remain silent. Do you understand this right? Anything you say can and will . . .”

I grab my phone and call Martin.

IT TAKES ALL DAY, but Martin finally gets Genevieve released on bail. They arrested her after finding what they claim is the murder weapon. A rock from Genevieve’s garden. There aren’t any clear prints on it, just partial, but there is a smidge of Harrison’s blood and hair from when it struck him in the head. And since the rock is from her garden, they felt it was enough to bring her in officially.

It wasn’t.

And Martin made sure everyone was aware of that when she went before the judge. It’s amazing how quickly high-profile cases get handled when the authorities want them to be.

A condition of Genevieve’s bail was a modified house arrest, so she’s wearing an ankle monitor to ensure she doesn’t go anywhere she’s not supposed to. She gets a 5-mile radius from home. She walks sluggishly toward the house, shaking her left leg every so often to situate the monitor.

“It’s going to be okay,” I remind her. She doesn’t respond. I know she’s shocked and upset. I don’t blame her. We get in the house, and I open a bottle of wine to pour her a glass. Hoping it will calm her a bit. “There’s no proof, Genevieve.”

She spins to face me. “What does it matter? They still arrested me. Everyone thinks I did it. I can’t prove I didn’t. The police know we slept together last night, that part was obvious. Which just lends to their belief I’m guilty. Can you just see the headlines: ‘Genevieve Daniels kills husband to be with ex-lover,' or 'Genevieve Daniels has ex-lover help with investigation when she's the suspect.'

I hang my head in shame, knowing I was instrumental in that. "I'm sorry. That was my fault."

"I wanted it just as much as you did," she says. "There's no one to blame."

"We figure out how to access the surveillance videos and get them submitted, it's a no brainer, babe. Al is working on the access now."

"I hope he knows what he's doing."

"Al's a woman, baby. No one's better than her."

"Oh."

I know that look. I've talked about Al quite a bit and even flirted with her a little over the phone in front of Genevieve. I shouldn't be surprised that she's jealous

"Genevieve, Al's not, uh, anyone I mess with. I mean we have, but we *don't*, we're just friends, okay?"

"You slept with her?"

"I've slept with a lot of women in the past four years."

"Oh, my god, I can't do this." She sinks to the ground and buries her head between her knees.

"Did you think I just stopped having sex because you weren't available?" Part of me means to piss her off when I say that. "It sure as fuck didn't stop you." And that.

"Are you kidding me right now?"

"No."

"I didn't have a choice!" she screams.

"You absolutely had a choice."

"You were gone."

"It was my job!" I yell.

She buries her face in her hands and sobs.

"You knew I would come back, Genevieve. I always did."

"I made a mistake," she cries. "A stupid, stupid mistake."

I sit on the floor next to her and pull her into my lap. "Shhh. It's okay."

She buries her face in my chest and clings to my shirt, her tears dampening the fabric. "I can't do this, Ty. I can't believe I killed Harrison. I can't go to jail for it."

"Well first darlin', it would be prison, not jail."

She laughs, despite herself.

"Second, I believe the videos will show you didn't do it."

She looks up and sniffles. "Do you really?"

"Yeah, really."

She takes a deep, shuddering breath, letting it out slowly. "And Al can get us the videos?"

"She's working on it as we speak."

Genevieve nods and stands, moving into the kitchen. "What's this?" she asks, pointing to the certified letter that was delivered today. "Oh, now I see. it's from Grant. Harrison's attorney."

She opens it and pulls out a sheath of paper. "It's a letter from Harrison. And his last will and testament."

I head to the patio to give her space to read it in private. I don't want to intrude on a private moment. But stay close enough to hear her in case she calls out. She goes through the pages one by one, tears streaming down her face.

18

————

Genevieve

Last Will and Testament of Harrison Benjamin Daniels

BE IT KNOWN, that I, Harrison Daniels, of Lake Oswego, Oregon, in the County of Clackamas in the State of Oregon, being of sound mind, do make, publish and declare this to be my Last Will and Testament, hereby revoking all my prior Wills and Codicils at any time made.

FIRST: I direct my Personal Representative, herein named, to pay all my just debts and funeral expenses as soon as may be convenient.

SECOND: To my daughters: Eerie Shelley Daniels and Curious Raven Daniels, I bequeath the sums of twenty-five thousand dollars a month to be paid in perpetuity upon their graduation from an accredited university after acquiring degrees in a field outside of the social sciences with minimum grade point averages of 3.0. Said education will be paid for in its entirety, from separate funds set aside for this sole purpose and to be executed by my Personal Representative.

THIRD: All the rest, residue, and remainder of my estate, whether real, personal or mixed property, of whatsoever situate (herein referred to as my "residuary estate"), I give, devise and bequeath to Genevieve Bujold Daniels, in total and without exception.

FOURTH: In the event that Genevieve Bujold Daniels, shall die with me, predecease me or not live beyond forty-eight hours after my death, I then give, devise and bequeath my estate in its entirety to Eerie Shelley Daniels and Curious Raven Daniels to be split evenly between them. or their issue per stirpes.

FIFTH: I hereby nominate, constitute, and appoint Grant Carter Show, my Personal Representative of this my Last Will and Testament, to act without bond.

I DON'T READ beyond the fifth point, there's no need to. Everything I need to know is in points one, two, three, and four. I motion Ty forward and hand it to him before sinking in a chair at the table and trying to collect my thoughts.

Harrison left me a literal fortune. And I have no idea what to do with it.

I pick up my phone and try to call the girls again. Eerie and Curious. They aren't talking to me, and I don't know why. Tyler mentioned they haven't spoken to the police yet either, which I'm surprised by. And apparently the police haven't pushed for an interview with them. Why not? Surely the girls will say I didn't kill Harrison, right?

I understand they're in shock and hurt. But why are they blocking me out? Unless they believe I'm guilty. By now, if I got a copy of Harrison's will, they probably did too. I can't imagine they are too happy about how things settled out. If I were them, I wouldn't be.

But they weren't talking to me before that. Why? I figured at a time like this they would want us all to be together.

I let the phone ring for a while. And let out a sigh when it goes to voicemail again.

"Hi, girls. It's me again. Can you please call me? I just want to know you're okay. I'm worried about you. Just let me know that you're okay. Please."

I wonder if I should call again and hope they answer this time. I mean they haven't in the last two days, but maybe this time would be different.

What's the definition of insanity, Genevieve?

I laugh to myself and put the phone down on the table.

With the amount of times I've tried to call the girls and it's gone to voicemail, I know they're listening to my messages. Otherwise, there wouldn't be space for me to continue leaving them. Which means one thing. They are avoiding me.

I even called Sarah this morning hoping she would let me know that the girls are okay. But that went straight to voicemail as well, so none of them want to talk to me.

I suppose I'm alone when it comes to family. Not that they were ever truly my family.

Which just leaves one person in my corner.

Tyler.

19

———————

Tyler

Once again, I sleep the entire night through with Genevieve in my arms. We haven't talked about anything yet. Not us. Not us fucking. Nothing. I know I'm okay picking up where we left off. I'd give it another chance. Genie's always been my one who got away. Problem is, I'm still not convinced I'm hers.

But I'm up this early because Martin finally got the warrant for the tapes, which took way longer than either one of us thought it would. It was back and forth for a while, but Martin told them it would have all the footage of what happened that night. I was surprised the judge didn't agree straight away. I'm meeting him at his office so the tech guy from the security company can "officially" look things up for us.

I wait for the tech guy to set up the replays for us, there are a few things I want to check and the first is the bedroom. If Genevieve was there all night, it's going to give me half the answers I need.

"There's nothing here," the tech guy says.

"What do you mean, there's nothing there?" I ask, my tone brusque.

"You wanted the fourteenth, right?"

"Yeah."

"It's all been wiped," he says.

"What do you mean, wiped?" I ask, feeling stupid that I just keep repeating everything he says.

"Deleted. Wiped. Gone."

"Can you get it back? Is there a backup? Who deleted it? It was just there."

"You saw it?" the tech guy asks.

"Yes."

"Well, why didn't you look at it then?" the tech guy asks.

"It was password protected," I say.

"Hmm," he says.

"Can you use recovery software to get it back since it hasn't been overwritten?" Martin asks.

The tech guy pulls on his beard in a rhythmic manner, like he's thinking. "Maybe, I'll have to check with the office and see."

"Do that," I say.

He grabs his phone and makes a call.

I move to stand next to Martin. "Someone deleted it."

"Who?" he asks.

"I don't know. But the ex-wife showed when I was there checking things out."

"Did she say or do anything?" he asks.

"No, but she was acting kind of weird. Claimed she wanted to make sure Daniels was dead."

Martin's brow furrows.

"And," I add. "She had a key."

"To the Lake Oswego house?" he confirms.

"Yeah."

"Well, she did live there once upon a time, I'm surprised Harrison didn't take it away."

"I'm sure he did, but I'm also sure the girls had a key."

"Good point," Martin says.

"Uh, sir?" the tech guy calls out.

I turn toward him. "Yeah?"

"So, we can recover it, it's going to take a little time and I have to wait for the office to upload the software I need so I can download it."

"How long is a little time?" I ask.

"Couple hours."

"Get on it," Martin says.

Martin and I leave to grab some coffee at the deli near his office.

"How's Genevieve?" Martin asks.

"Freaking out. Harrison's twins won't call her back. She's convinced they think she's guilty."

"I meant, how are you with Genevieve."

"Fine. Why do you ask?"

"Really, Ty?"

I shake my head. "I fucked her." Then rub my face with my hands.

Martin just nods, like he was expecting it.

"What?" I ask.

"You still love her," he says.

"So?"

"So, there's still a slim chance she's guilty. Be careful."

I shake my head. "Nah, man. I don't think she's got it in her."

Martin shrugs.

"Don't do that. Not my dick talking."

"Okay," he says. "I just want to make sure you're looking out for number one."

"Aw, shucks, didn't know you cared," I tease.

"Who says I meant you?' He teases back.

We get back to the office. I hand the tech guy the coffee I brought back for him.

"It's gone faster than we thought," he says. "We should be able to access the files in the next few minutes."

I nod.

He flushes.

Either he digs me, or I make him nervous. Both thoughts make me chuckle.

"I got it," the tech guy says.

"Fucking finally," I say under my breath, rolling my eyes. It's only been two hours longer than I'd anticipated at this point.

"Thank you," Martin says.

We join him back at the conference table where he has his laptop set up.

"Okay, which room?" the tech guy asks.

"All of them," I say.

"Let's start with the master bedroom," Martin says.

"Go slow," I instruct. "And if I say stop, you better fucking stop." I'm hoping there's not a repeat of Genevieve getting herself off.

There is.

This girl.

Fuck my life.

I cover the screen with my hands. "Both of you close your eyes," I tell the tech guy and Martin.

They do.

"I'm going to fast forward through this part." Both men nod in response.

One thing's for sure, my girl has a healthy sexual appetite outside of her time with Harrison. I fast forward through her getting herself off and calling out my name. Again. Willing my dick not to harden and my chest not to swell with pride.

We get past the initial awkwardness, and the guy goes through the entire recording of the night of the murder. It quickly becomes clear; Genevieve did not leave her bed the entire time. Relief floods through me. At the very least, we know she didn't do it.

Now to find out who did.

We review the remainder of the house for the rest of the night. Nothing.

"Pull up the exterior footage for that night," I instruct, not taking my eyes off the screen.

The tech guy starts clicking on the keyboard, moving the video forward, and changing from one camera to another. "Stop."

What the fuck?

"Go back a few minutes and start it again. Play it in slow motion."

He does as I instruct. I take note of the time and watch the scene unfold. It's like something out of a bad movie. Harrison is sitting on a chair at the edge of the pool having just finished his swim. His elbows rest on his knees and his head is hung down. My guess is, catching his breath after the workout. Twin figures dressed all in black approach him from behind. He doesn't appear to hear them.

One hits him on the back of the head with a rock. The other pushes him back into the pool.

The water tinges pink around his head as he floats lifelessly, the wound on his head bleeding. The pair watch him for ninety-seven seconds before heading toward the house, rock still in hand. Something to the left catches their attention, and they pause before running out of the camera's frame.

"Find where they went," I tell the tech guy. He scrolls through everything again, not finding them. Until he pulls up footage of the driveway, the two figures get into the back seat of a dark-colored BMW before it pulls away from the far side of the house.

I pace the room trying to work out what's happened.

"Martin, work this out with me. What do we know for sure? Two people killed him. A third person drove the car. BMW."

Martin gets up and grabs a pen from the whiteboard on the wall and writes:

- *two murderers*
- *one driver*
- *erased surveillance footage*
- *BMW*

"We know the ex-wife has a key to the house," I continue.

"Maybe she erased it then," the tech guy says laughing.

It hits me like a load of bricks. "What's your name, again?" I ask him.

"Eddie," he says.

"Eddie, you're a fucking genius."

He flushes under my praise.

"Can we get access to her erasing what she erased in the same way we got what she erased?"

"I think so?" Eddie looks at me, quizzically, saying it more like a question than a statement.

"There's no surveillance in the safe room, right?" I confirm.

"No," Eddie says.

"But there is in Harrison's office, which is where the door to the safe room is," Martin adds, understanding where I'm going with this.

"Exactly," I say. "Is there a way to know when the original recordings were erased?"

"You mean, like a date?" Eddie asks.

"Yes," I say.

"No," he says.

"Okay, let's try footage from yesterday and the day before."

It takes a while, but we finally hit paydirt with Sarah Daniels going back to the house yesterday. She accessed the safe room, was there for close to ten minutes, then left.

"She fucking erased the footage," I say to no one in particular.

"Would appear that way," Eddie adds unnecessarily.

"We have two killers, similar height and body type. And one mom who erased the proof. Sound like anyone we know?" I ask unnecessarily. Then turn to Martin. "What do we do now?"

"Doesn't change much," he says. "Whether we're using the original or a recovered file, the images are still the same. We got two hooded killers and one clear as day accomplice."

I nod in response.

Now to find definitive proof.

I TRY to call Genevieve on my way back to the beach house, but she doesn't answer. I speed up the tiniest bit. Not yet worried that something has happened, but not feeling entirely comfortable with not being able to reach Genevieve either.

"Genevieve?" Nothing looked out of the ordinary when I pulled up to the house. Now that I'm inside, the same applies.

Still, no Genevieve.

Where the fuck did she go?

That's when I see the note on the kitchen island.

T – the girls finally called me back!
   We're going to the Seaside Festival today. I'll be back later.
   Love, G
   PS – Phone died. No time to charge it before leaving.

Aw, what the fuck, Genevieve? What part of don't go anywhere does she not understand?

I hit up Al.

"Hey handsome," she answers.

"Can you hack an ankle bracelet monitor?"

"If you could see me now, I'm rolling my eyes."

"Can you send live feeds to my phone?" I ask.

"No. But I can access the live feed and give you updates."

I give her the registration number for Genevieve's ankle bracelet and wait for her to confirm she has it.

"Got it," she says.

"Where is it now?"

"Fairgrounds. In, Seaside."

"I know that," I say drily. "Can you pinpoint?"

"You didn't ask that," she says.

I hear her typing rapidly, and then, "South end. That's the best I can do."

"You're the best," I tell her.

"I know," she says before disconnecting.

I hit up Martin again. "She's at the Seaside Festival with the twins. South end of the fairgrounds according to an anonymous source. I think she's in danger. Can you get police backup?"

"I'll do my best."

I feel like I'm losing my fucking edge. Can't think straight where this girl is concerned. "Thanks, man. Heading out there now."

"Keep in touch."

"Will do."

20

Genevieve

ONE HOUR BEFORE

I'm just coming in from outside when the doorbell rings. Which I find odd since I'm not expecting anyone, and Ty has a key. I smile when I see two faces I've been wanting to see since this nightmare began.

"Girls! Oh, my goodness, I've been trying to call you for days." I give them both a hug for longer than I probably should. They return it, but it feels odd, almost reluctant. I'm excited to see them because I assume it means they don't think I'm guilty, but maybe that's not the case.

"We know," Eerie says. "We needed time."

"To process this," Curious adds.

It always freaks me out a bit when the girls finish one another's thoughts or sentences. According to Harrison, they've done it since childhood.

"We're sorry we left you when you needed us." They both sound like they're reading from a script. "You needed us to support you, and we weren't there."

"We're super sorry." The monotone of their voices throws me off.

Then it hits me. They think I did it. And they are forcing themselves to come here for their dad's sake.

"Never mind all that. I'm just so happy that you're here now," I say. "I kept calling because I wanted to make sure you knew I didn't kill your dad. I would never do anything like that. You know how much I loved him." I look to them for reassurance. They don't say anything. Don't even look at me.

"Okay, well, let's go sit down." I gesture awkwardly to the living room. Not knowing how to feel based on their attitudes. "How are you? I mean, outside of the obvious." I try to temper my enthusiasm at seeing them and keep my tone in check. I know we're all grieving here and even though it's such a relief for me to see them, it may not be the same feeling for them.

"Is it okay if we aren't . . . *here*?" Curious asks. "It's just too hard with all these reminders of Daddy."

"Daddy?" I laugh. They've never called him that before. They don't laugh with me. "Yes, of course. Let me get my purse. Do you just want to go to the coffee shop down the street or something?"

"We were thinking maybe the Seaside Festival," Eerie says. "In honor of him and all."

One of Harrison's more popular books, *Summer Shivers*, featured a serial killer carnie on the carnival circuit. He would kill people in all sorts of different ways in each city the carnival set up in. Authorities never put together the crimes were happening by the same person or whenever the carnival was in town. The carnie went on to kidnap a girl and bring her on the road with him. He impregnated the girl and killed her after his son was born. Then raised the child to follow in his footsteps. It's a gory tale to be sure, but it was a bestseller. The festival has a Fun House dedicated to the book featuring interactions with the victims.

"Sure, yeah. Give me one sec." I grab a sweater to pair with my maxi sundress in case it gets cold. I put on a long dress this morning, so I didn't have to look at my ankle bracelet. Which works out since I am leaving the house. No need to advertise it's there if I don't have to.

I grab my phone to send Ty a text and see that it's totally dead. I plug it in and write him a note instead, leaving it on the kitchen counter where he'll see it first thing.

I lock up and follow them to their car, excited to finally tell them my side of the story, hoping they believe me.

"How are you both?" I ask as we get in the car—me in the backseat, Curious driving, and Eerie in the passenger seat.

They look at each other before speaking. "I still can't believe this happened," Eerie starts. "I mean, I always thought Daddy would be here all the time."

"For our wedding day," Curious adds.

"To play with his grandkids." Eerie stops for a moment to wipe the tears from under her eyes. "I never thought something like this could happen." Her voice is soft, and shaky.

I just want to give them both a hug and promise it will be okay. "I'm so sorry. I know how hard it is to lose a husband. I can only imagine what it's like to lose a dad." I say this even though I know what it's like to lose a dad. My parents died when I was young, so they didn't have as large an impact on my life as maybe Harrison did on the twins. But I know what it's like to not have one around for sure. I don't point that out, though. I get the feeling they don't want me empathizing with them and that they'd like to be left alone in their grief. I'm happy to let them be if it means they'll talk to me again.

Not that we were ever *that* close. But I think it would be important to Harrison that I maintain a relationship with them. So, I will.

We ride in silence for a few more minutes. Which I start to find bothersome. I mean, if they didn't want to talk, why reach out at all?

"How's your mom?" I ask, trying to get them to open up to me.

"Mom hasn't really said anything," Curious says. "She's just quiet most of the time."

I think about Sarah's interaction with Ty at the Lake Oswego house and wonder how she's handling it. The two were married for about fifteen years and their divorce was bitter. But they seemed to grow more amicable over the years as the girls grew older. I'm sure she's sad about it. He's still the father of her children.

We pull into the dirt lot where people park for the festival and head in to the fairgrounds. In addition to rides and a food court, there's also various vendor exhibits and presentations. I pay for our admission and buy a bunch of ride tickets for the girls. I don't plan to go on any rides, but I'm sure they'll want to.

"Let's hit the *Summer Shivers* Fun House first," Curious says. I agree. It's not a ride, it's the main reason we're here, and I'm sure the girls are anxious to have the reminder of their dad. The closer we get, the more nervous I feel. But I can't put my finger on why.

The girls have friends in line already. Despite my protests, the girls cut in to join them. So, I do too. I hand some of the people behind us ride tickets as an apology.

Eerie nudges her friend and jerks her chin toward me, rolling her eyes.

What's that about?

I'm just trying to be nice.

The line moves forward a few steps, I go to follow when something jerks me back. The collar of my dress rides up my chest, making it press at my windpipe.

Hard.

I can't breathe.

My hands fly to my throat in a panic, pulling at the neckline trying to loosen it. It just grows tighter. I can't seem to move, caught too off guard.

I try to slap at Curious to get her attention.

"What?" She spins to face me, her tone vicious. Then seeing me claw at my neck, she looks behind me and says, "Derek, dude, get off my *stepmom's* dress. You're choking her." I turn to see a boy pick his foot off the back hem of my dress. My breathing returns to normal.

What the hell?

He looks over his shoulder at us. "My bad. Sorry." Then turns back to his conversation like it was nothing. I rub at my neck, sure there's a line there now from the thin, cotton edging around the neck of my dress. I know it was an accident, but I still feel weird about it.

Like something odd is going on.

Why did Eerie roll her eyes at me? And Curious have that tone?

I feel like they're upset and I'm not sure I feel comfortable with them. I wish I had my cell phone with me. I could call Ty and ask him to come get me.

Ha, if I thought the girls had an issue with me now, just wait until they see Ty picking me up. That won't go over well at all.

"Hey, girls, I think I'm going to sit this one out," I say as we climb the steps toward the entrance to the 'ride.'

"No way, Genevieve." Eerie grabs my arm and pulls me along with her. "We are doing this together. As a *family*."

I go along. Because, really, what else can I do? She said family. I'll feel like a jerk if I don't participate. The girls must be upset over their dad's death and acting out a bit. I can't blame them for that. They are barely out of their teens at a year shy of twenty.

We're herded into a narrow, darkened corridor just past the entrance of the Fun House. The bodies of the girls and their friends tighten around me. Jostling me back and forth.

Hard.

It's like I don't have control over where I go and am just being forced along by the small crowd surrounding me. It's an unsettling feeling.

"Can we spread out a bit?" I ask.

I can hear their snickers in response. Even though no one responds. Are they crowding me on purpose? I'm pushed roughly to one side – bumping hard into what I think is the wall.

Panic sets in. I don't like feeling out of control.

"Curious? Eerie?"

Neither girl answers.

The space around us is pitch black. I can't see what's in front of me. Their bodies close in further. I feel suffocated. I don't like having this many people so close to me. Even if two of them are my stepdaughters.

A maniacal laughter sounds off from the Fun House, making me jump. I know it's for effect but that doesn't make it any less creepy. My imagination runs a bit wild, and I can't help the fear that closes in.

I don't like that I can't see anywhere around me.

I'm not comfortable in such a confined space.

"Girls?"

Why aren't they answering me?

If they believe I killed their father, why ask me to join them at the festival? Why not continue to ignore my calls?

Maybe they're trying to get back at you.

By what, Genevieve, scaring you to death?

I try to laugh off my thoughts. But my heart is pounding radically in my chest. I hate this feeling of not knowing what's going on. Growing up in foster care, you never really know what's going to happen from one day to the next. Will you remain in the home? Will you get moved to another? Might this be the day you are finally adopted. It creates such a desire for some semblance of control, that it's hard to continue life without it. I close my eyes for a moment and focus on relaxing my body and my mind.

The stress surrounding me starts to dissipate.

Just a little scare. No big deal.

Oddly, nothing had really shown up in the Fun House yet. We've just been in a maze of dark corridors. I thought it was more a tour of all the fictional victims.

As though I've summoned it, strobe lights start, blinding me with their brightness. Faces pop into my periphery at random. I can't tell if they are real or fake. The maniacal laughter sounds off again. I feel around with my hands but can't touch anything. It's disorienting.

I close my eyes and try to center myself. It's just a space for amusement at a festival. Nothing here can harm you. Harrison's lifeless body pops into my mind. With his gaping mouth and vacant stare.

It's just a memory. It can't hurt you either.

In—two, three, four.

Hold—three, two one.

Out—two, three four.

Calm. Center. Breathe. Relax.

The lights stop, thrusting us back into total darkness.

My eyes can't adjust fast enough and all I see each time I blink are starbursts of color.

Whispers fill the air around me. Unintelligible, but everywhere at once, like they're touch us as they dance by.

Why did I agree to this? I've never been a fan of the dark. Hence the sleeping pills with wine. If I could be a day sleeper I'd do much better.

"Hello?" I call out. The Fun House operator would know if something nefarious was going on, right?

The whispers stop followed by a loud click, similar to how gallows sound in movies when releasing a body to hang.

Right on cue, a body drops from the ceiling directly in front of me, the torso slapping me in the face as it settles.

I can't stop the scream that escapes me. My hands flying out to push it away. The body is sticky, leaving some sort of residue on my face and hands. Then the buzzing starts.

I know instantly what it is.

Harrison's stories are beginning.

This one is a re-enactment from one of his earlier books. A modified hanging where the victim had just enough of a foothold to stay alive, but every time they moved, razor wire would slice their skin, resulting in a bloody, sticky mess. When they didn't bleed out fast enough the killer got upset with how long it was taking and released a bunch of flies in the room. They surrounded the still living victim, laid eggs, and well, suffice it to say there's a reason why Harrison was labeled the King of Horror.

I wipe my hands down the front of my dress and keep moving forward. Lights flicker to my right. A gory corpse stares at me with a mouth that is drawn open and eyes that are dead inside. Reminiscent of how Harrison looked when I found him in the pool.

Deep breaths.

In—two, three four.

Hold—three, two, one.

Out—two, three, four.

I continue to feel my way forward, unsure where the rest of the group went since it feels as though I'm alone in this now. Something pokes me in the side, I turn, but can't feel or see anything. The same thing happens on the other side. It feels like the end of a stick. Thin and blunt.

I turn again. "Hello?"

My voice echoes back at me. "Hello." Poked from the back.

"Hello." Poked from the side.

"Hello." The front.

The back.

The side.

Over and over. Each poke harder than the last. Feeling as though they'll leave bruises around the softer parts of my body. I try to fend them off with my hands but there are too many coming at me from all angles. The word 'hello' coming at me faster and faster until it merges together into one long hum. The pokes non-stop.

I don't think I can handle this.

A scream percolates in my throat.

I've got to get out of here.

I push my way forward, ending headfirst in a wall.

I turn to the opposite direction. Another wall.

That wasn't there before. Was it?

I reach my hands to the sides. Wall and wall. Then turn and do it again. Oh my god, I'm boxed in.

How did this happen?

I don't like small spaces.

"Help!" I cry out, not caring who hears me. Or if the kids make fun of me. I don't like this, and I want out. "Hello!"

The enclosure I've been boxed into tips forward. I put my hands out to stop my fall, but there's not enough space. My face hits hard. Pain explodes behind my eyes.

"Oh, fuck!"

Warm blood trickles down my chin.

I can't breathe. I touch my face gingerly; my nose doesn't feel quite right. Did I break it?

What the hell is going on?

I kick my feet out, trying to get purchase on the bottom. Something. Anything. They just hit air.

The pounding sounds with the box jostling in rhythm. Like someone is using a hammer and nails.

I kick out again and my feet hit resistance this time.

I've been closed in on the final side.

I'm in the box.

Totally surrounded.

Oh my god.

"Help!" I scream. This has gone way too far. "Help!"

The box tips again and begins to move. Feeling more likes it's rolling, as though on some sort of hand truck or dolly. The terrain changes from smooth to rough. I can hear the sounds of the carnival around us.

"Help! Someone please help! Hello?" I try banging on the inside of the box, but my hands don't have enough space to make barely a tap. "Hello!"

The noises from the outside fade away and the box stops.

"Curious? Eerie? Hello?"

I smell smoke. Not like the barbecue pit in the food court, more like leaves or trash that is on fire.

Thump. Thump. THUMP. Thump. Thump. THUMP. Thump. Thump. THUMP.

The banging on the outside of the box starts.

Thump. Thump. THUMP. Thump. Thump. THUMP. Thump. Thump. THUMP.

Like the beginning of that Queen song, making me want to sing. Which almost makes me laugh since when I would get scared as a kid, I would sing songs to feel better. And this is one that I would sing.

I try to do it now; my voice won't cooperate.

Thump. Thump. THUMP. Thump. Thump. THUMP. Thump. Thump. THUMP.

The smell of smoke intensifies.

"Hello?"

I hear the crackling of fire.

And I realize, they're going to burn me alive.

"HELP!!!!!! SOMEONE PLEASE!!!"

21

———————

Tyler

I've been through the entire fairgrounds and haven't found her. The police should be here soon with the tracker for her ankle bracelet. Until then, all I can do is hope I find them at the south end before anything happens.

"Fucks sake, Genevieve, where are you?"

When I see the *Summer Shivers* Fun House, I realize if she's going to be anywhere, it's there. I run toward it, best I can. My knee already sore from fucking Genevieve against the wall and in the shower, plus all the walking I've done lately. I should have worn my brace. Now, I'll pay the price with barely being able to walk later.

When I get there, I see a sign saying it's closed. I find a guy nearby and ask what happened.

"Some lady got hurt inside. Had to shut it down." He shrugs.

"Some lady? Do you know who?" I ask.

"No idea."

"Where would they take her?"

"First Aid tent back that way." He points to the entrance, a good half a mile from where I am now. Fuck my life.

I'm just getting to the entrance when the police arrive. I grab the lead detective, who I know from working past cases together. "Got a beat on her?"

"I'd say she's about a mile that way." He points to the far end of the fairgrounds, where I just was.

"The fairgrounds aren't that long," I say.

He shows me the screen. Sure as shit, that's what it looks like. "There a golf cart somewhere we can take?' I hate asking, but I'm not going to make it otherwise.

"Little cardio too much for you?" he jokes.

"You could say that. Busted kneecap in the service."

"Sorry, man. Let me see what I can do." He makes a request with his walkie-talkie and next thing I know a couple people pull up in golf carts to give us a ride. I gratefully sink to the bench seat on the back and rest my leg while we make our way through the crowds. Much slower than I would like, but faster than if I were walking. We hit the edge of the fairgrounds and exit through a gate beyond.

"You guys smell smoke?"

"Probably the BBQ pit," the guy driving the golf cart says.

"Nah, this is different," I tell him.

"You smell smoke?" I yell to the cops in the neighboring cart.

One nods. "Yeah."

We make our way through a bunch of trees to a small clearing where a group of teens sit chanting around a tall box, under which is a small fire.

"Genevieve?" I yell.

The kids start to scatter.

"Don't move!" the cops yell, firing a warning shot in the air. All the kids stop, and I'm off the cart and running toward the box before it's barely stopped.

I push the box over and drag it from the fire, kicking dirt on it and patting out the small flames with my hands.

"Genevieve!?"

"Ty? Oh god, Ty, is that you? Please help me! I'm burning!" I hear a small voice from inside the box.

"Cover your face, baby." I grab my Ka-Bar from my waistband and bust the box open from what I think is the side.

Genevieve starts pushing her hands through. "Get me out! Get me out!"

"I am, baby. Hang on." I pull the main front piece off and find Genevieve covered in blood.

I gather her in my arms. "Where are you bleeding?"

"It's my nose," she says. "They broke my nose." She sounds congested, so I believe it probably is broken. Her eyes are already starting to swell.

She pants for air and wraps her arms tightly around my neck, telling me, "Thank you," over and over again.

"What happened? You hurt anywhere else?"

"I don't think so." She buries her head in my chest. "They hate me, Ty. They think I killed Harrison."

I'm not sure if this is the right time to tell her what's going on or not. But there's probably no better time.

"They killed him, babe," I say.

She looks up at me through wet lashes. "What?" Shock blankets her face.

"We're pretty sure the video footage shows they killed their dad. Sarah knew and tried to cover for them by deleting it. It's why she was at the house that day."

"I don't understand."

The officers already have most of the kids in handcuffs. I help Genevieve stand and as she tries to steady herself on her feet so she can go talk to them.

The girls stare at us defiantly as we approach.

"Did you kill your dad?" she asks in disbelief.

One of them shrugs.

"Did you not know your dad had cameras in the whole house?" I ask.

They both look at each other.

"Not until after," the first one says to Genevieve. "Mom was supposed to take care of that."

"Lotta good that did us," the other one says. I can't tell the two girls apart. I'm sure Genevieve can. Not that I'm sure it matters at this point. Or if I care.

"Oh my god." Genevieve collapses against me but addresses them. "What have you done?"

"He was mean to mom. She deserved more. It wasn't fair," the first one says.

"Me, Eerie, and Mom had a plan; we were going to kill you, too," the other one says. Guess that makes her Curious. "We needed the money," she continues.

"But someone got a little too anxious and hit dad over the head with a rock instead of following the plan," Eerie adds.

"It worked, didn't it?" Curious sneers.

"Do you call this working?"

"You and Mom had a stupid plan," Curious says.

"Like you could do better!" Eerie throws back. "I'm going to tell her you said that."

"Doesn't matter now, idiot." Curious rolls her eyes.

～

GENEVIEVE BREATHES in deeply and lets it out slowly, shaking her head in disbelief. "How could you do this?" she asks them.

"You wouldn't understand," Eerie says. "You don't have to worry about money."

"Mom's book wasn't doing well," Curious adds. "Thanks to Dad."

"Don't get us wrong, you seemed really nice in the beginning," Eerie says.

"We were always doing family meals and you were always making sure that we'd come around to see Dad, so he spent time with us," Curious adds. "But then Dad got busy, and Mom ran out of money. You decided to have a baby, and everything changed. Dad wanted us to go to college if we wanted to keep getting our money—"

"You mean, *his* money," Genevieve interjects. They ignore her.

"And every time we talked to him," Eerie continues. "It was all Genevieve this and Genevieve that. Princess Fucking Genevieve who can do no wrong. The rest of us didn't exist anymore."

"Mom needed money. Dad abandoned her. You were going to take *our* money. We had no choice," the first one says.

"We knew once the new baby came, we were going to be old news," Curious adds. It's amazing how they can carry on a contiguous conversation, completing one another's thoughts like that.

"We have to be able to live," Eerie says.

"And Mom needs us," Curious finishes.

"Why did you think we were already having a baby?" Genevieve asks. I see more cop cars pull up in my periphery.

"Dad said you were, and we were like that's not happening," Eerie says.

"You're already kicking us out for her. What are you going to do when a baby comes along?" Curious shouts as though she's talking to her dad.

"We weren't even pregnant," Genevieve screams back. I'm relieved to finally hear anger from her. It means she's fighting back.

"But Dad said—" Eerie starts.

Genevieve shakes her head. "You've got it all wrong. We were talking about it, yes. And sometimes trying, sure. We both thought we're at a good place to bring *another* child in to grow the family and bring us all together." Tears stream down her face, but her voice stays strong.

"You killed your dad, and you were about to kill me because you didn't want to share your dad's love or his money." Genevieve almost whispers the last part. "What kind of monsters are you?"

"You're the monster," Eerie says.

"We're not monsters," Curious adds. "We're survivors. Fuck you, Genevieve."

"Yeah, fuck you," Eerie chimes in.

"Alright, let's go." The officers collectively grab the girls by their cuffs and direct them toward the backseats of the patrol cars.

They did this out of greed. Whether for money or their dad's love, I'm not sure. Completely fucked up when people who are raised with everything still want more.

"Let's go see if we can get that fucking bracelet off, and then I'll take you home."

"Thank you for not giving up on me." She leans up, giving me a chaste kiss on the lips.

I cock my brow. "You call that a thank you?"

She giggles. It's fan-fucking-tastic to hear again. "No, I'll give you the real thank you later. Consider that like the virginal version of what's to come."

"Looking forward to the non-virginal version then."

"X-rated," she whispers.

"Like that even more."

She takes my hand in hers, and I let her, as we stroll toward the detective, ready to get this over with.

22

———

Tyler

It takes at least two hours longer than I anticipate for Genevieve to give her statement, get the charges dropped, and get her fucking ankle bracelet removed. We also have her looked at by a doctor, luckily her nose isn't broken, but it'll be pretty sore for a while and her eyes will still blacken a bit.

"Why don't you go take a shower, and I'll open you a bottle of wine and put together a snack," I tell her.

"I would like that," she says.

I open the wine, light the fireplace, dim the bulb lighting, put on some light blues music, and attempt to arrange a platter of whatever shit she has in the fridge. Not gonna lie, not my forte. Ends up looking like what it is: a pile of leftovers all slung together.

I set everything up in the living room. Going for romance. Hoping I succeed. She deserves it. Plan to fuck her brains out tonight. I'm going crazy after almost losing her. Again. But, need her to feel wooed, too.

"Wow, what's all this?" she asks, coming into the room in a short silk robe.

"Called taking your mind off the shit that was today," I say.

"I like it."

I hand her a glass of wine, then move to stand behind her rubbing her shoulders and the back of her neck gently. Trying to work out some of the stress kinks.

"Oh, that feels good," she moans, melting back against me.

We continue like that for a moment, then she sets her wine down and turns around to face me. Looking like she wants to say something. "They were nineteen. How do you decide at such a young age that you're going to kill someone and then do it?"

"Happens. Even at younger ages. World can be a fucked up place." I grab my whiskey and take a large gulp, relishing the burn as it slides down my throat.

"It feels different somehow when you know the killer."

I nod in agreement.

"Can we talk?" she asks.

"Thought we were," I tease.

"I'm sorry I didn't tell you I was pregnant."

"I know you are."

"Can you forgive me?"

"Already have."

"Really?" She looks surprised by that.

I set my whiskey down by her wine glass and take her hands in mine. Raising each one to my mouth and kissing it before continuing. "Yeah. I mean, I'm still hurt by it, but I understand why you did it. It was a shitty time for us. I get that you couldn't reach me. And I don't blame you for panicking and turning to Harrison."

"Thank you."

"Do blame him for coercing you to marry him. I don't blame him for loving you. Who wouldn't love you?" I cup her cheek in my palm, she leans into it. "Never stopped loving you, babe."

Her face softens. "Do you think we have a chance?" she asks.

"I do."

"I never stopped loving you either," she whispers.

"Knew that when I found out you thought of me when you fucked him."

She blushes. "And other times."

"Pink dildo and the little red vibrator?"

Her eyes widen. "How did you—"

"Cameras in the bedroom."

"Oh my god." She buries her head in her hands. "I didn't—"

I pull her hands away from her face. "No reason to be embarrassed. It was fucking hot to watch."

"Oh yeah?" she asks, coyly. "Maybe I can do a reenactment sometime."

"Fuck yes. Know what else I want to reenact?" I ask. I wait until she meets my eyes again, then I kiss her. A soft kiss at first, 'cause I know she likes those.

I instantly need more. When I hear her moan, I take it. Pushing my tongue into her mouth, I pour everything I'm feeling into this kiss. The passion, the longing, the love.

I give it all to her, not stopping until I'm so out of breath I feel lightheaded. I pull my lips away, chest heaving

"Need you," I rasp.

"Yes," she breathes.

I untie the belt on her robe and push it from her shoulders to pool at the floor. She stands before me, naked and exquisite. I lean in to kiss a few of the bruises from the fucking savages poking her with sticks and broom handles. I work my way around her body kissing them all softly. Trying to show how sorry I am, even if it's not my fault.

She reaches down as I'm kissing her shoulder and pulls my shirt up from the hem. I reach behind my neck to get it the rest of the way off. Her hands graze my bare chest, fingers sliding through the hair there, giggling when my abs contract at her touch.

I let her explore.

Until it's my turn.

I push her back against the couch and move to kneel in front of her. Spreading her legs wide apart, her pussy glistens in the firelight. She drops them open even further, an invitation I'm not even sure she realizes she's giving. I take my time, start with kisses on the insides of her ankles and the bottoms of her feet. She gasps in response, jerking her leg back when I hit a part that is ticklish or sensitive. I move my hands up her calves to the backs of her knees, my lips soon following. Kissing and licking the skin as I go. My tongue leaving a trail of wetness in its wake. I palm her thighs, spreading her legs impossibly wide, before burying my nose in her pussy and breathing in deeply.

"Fuck, you smell so good," I groan. I lick the folds surrounding her clit. My tongue dipping in to fuck her entrance, allowing myself a hint of what I'll be feasting on soon. Her hands come around my head to hold it in place.

"Please," she begs.

I flatten my tongue against her and lick her hard. Her body writhes as I hit the end of her clit and suck. Her hands pull me in closer. It's all I can not to devour her. She wraps her legs around my head, a sign as far as I'm concerned that screams all systems go. My mouth engulfs her like I've never eaten before and fear I never will again. She cries out my name, making me grunt in satisfaction. Her first orgasm is quick to happen. Her body tensing and bucking as she comes all over my face. I slurp at her juices as they flow out of her, coating my lips and chin. My hips attempt to fuck the base of the couch, my cock desperate for a release. I need her to come again, if not two or three more times.

I slide two fingers inside her, crooking them slightly to find that sweet spot. Then I flicker her clit with my tongue, getting both at the same time. She's so tight, so wet. Her muscles clamp down around my fingers, her cries grow louder. "Oh, my god, Ty. Oh, god."

My thumb inches toward her ass and pushes it way in when I find that puckered hole.

Her thighs clamp around my head, hands pulling my mouth against her as she screams, undulating through her release. Her hips up, head thrown back, body straight as a board as she lets it roll through her, and she looks amazing doing it.

She begins to sob. "Oh, god, oh, god."

"You okay?"

"It's good cries. Good cries." I place her feet gently on the floor, before wiping her excess come off my face with my hands. She curls into herself on the couch.

"Too much. It's too much, I can't." She's panting.

"Nowhere near done, babe."

We can't be. Want this every day. Time between her legs, giving her pleasure, feeling her thighs tighten, her muscles spasm, hearing her cries, tasting her release.

"So fucking beautiful." I reach my hand out to caress her cheek. She leans into my palm, then grabs it to pull me toward her to run her tongue over my lips.

"I like the taste of me on you," she says.

"Makes two of us."

She sits up, her hands go to my waistband, unfastening my jeans and slowly pulling down the zipper. I'm so hard, the tip of my dick is peeking out the top of my boxer briefs. She pushes my pants down my legs, moving with them, until she's face level with my crotch. She leans in and runs her cheek against my cock. Starting at her cheekbone, then circling around to the front, her tongue slipping out to lick the tip, then back up the other side of the cheek.

"There'll be time for that later," I say, standing to shed the rest of my clothes before stretching out next to her on the couch. "Got plans. Plan to have you riding my face a lot. Plan to let you return the favor. Right now though, got plans for other things."

23

Genevieve

Ty hovers over me, nudging my hair to the side with his chin and running his tongue along the side of my neck, biting lightly. I run my fingers through his hair as I pull his lips back to mine. He settles his weight down, rubbing his hard cock against my center. He groans as we touch. I feel it between my legs. He sounds so raw and primal. I'm ready for him, aching for him.

"Ty, I need you inside me."

My body trembles with desire. I'm impatient, on edge, even after orgasming like I did. Like I'm on the precipice of something huge, and all I need is a little push.

"Taking my time, babe," he says.

"No," I whine, wiggling my hips under him to get his cock inside me.

"Slow down, tiger." He chuckles.

"Slow down later." I reach between us and grab him. Running my hand from one thick hot end to the other.

"Keep that up, I won't make it bein' inside you."

I rub the tip against my clit. "Feels so good, Ty."

He moans again. I love that sound. I lean forward and kiss him. He lets me control it for a moment before taking over. Kissing me, again and again, until my head is spinning and I'm certain I'll never be able to catch my breath. He tastes incredible, like whiskey and man, making me dizzy with desire.

"Please," I moan against his lips as his rough hands run over my skin. It feels so good, he feels so good. I'm going to die. This will kill me.

He runs his nose along mine softly, breath heavy against my face. My body trembles with need.

"I want to make this last forever." He kisses his way down my body and wedges his broad shoulders between my thighs. "Want you to come again."

"I can't," I say weakly.

"You can," he says, running one rough hand down from my breast to my navel and then between my legs. He parts my folds with his fingers and slowly rubs my clit with one. His rough fingers feel delicious against my soft skin. I flex my hips against him, a nonverbal invitation to give me more. His fingers move up and down sliding through my wetness. He pushes three fingers into me, and I arch into his hand.

"Oh, god, it hurts so good."

He chuckles. "I'll kiss it and make it better."

I grip the sheets with one hand, and his head with the other, pushing it down closer to where I want it to be. He adds his tongue with his fingers. The sensations are overwhelming. Scissoring his fingers. Spreading me wider. Filling me further Tearing me apart. Soothing with his tongue.

I feel so full, so close to exploding. I barely have time to think about the fourth finger entering my ass before his lips pull at my clit. My hips buck. I can't get enough.

I need him to stop.

I need him closer.

He pushes his nose deeply into me and groans, "Fuck, your pussy is delicious." His mouth engulfs me. My eyes close, my body goes loose, letting sensation take over.

"Oh, god. Oh, shit. Ty!"

He takes his arm and pins my hips down, his long fingers digging into my skin, holding me still.

I'm panting, breathless, my body overheated, trembling uncontrollably.

I can't take anymore.

Tongue and fingers swirling and licking, pulling and pushing until I can't tell which is what. My body tenses, my head comes up, trying to see him at the same time as feel him. His fingers pulsing against the walls of my vagina, his mouth sucking on my clit, his thumb entering my ass.

My body responds with a mind of its own, as I'm thrown into an abyss of pure pleasure. Total hedonistic abandon. My vision blurs, body convulses, I can't breathe. My nails dig into his scalp as I scream through my release, coming harder than I ever have before.

He gives me no reprieve to come down. Instead, blanketing my body with his as he works his hips between my legs, stretching them wide. I get no warning as he thrusts into me in one swoop.

"Oh god!" I cry out.

He moves his hands down to my hips, fingertips gripping my ass cheeks, to pull me in closer. I'm hungry for him. Already.

I raise my head to bite at his neck, hard.

His resulting moan almost as satisfying as his dick. To

know that I can make this man feel and lose control. His lips move across my mouth to my neck, biting and sucking. He's going to leave a mark, and I don't care. All I care about is him and the relief his cock is going to bring.

He reaches up to grab my tits, bringing them together, biting both nipples at the same time. For the first time, in a long time, I feel alive from the top of my head to the tips of my toes.

"Fuck you hard, babe. You're going to come again," he warns, then takes my hips and plunges back in. I can't help but cry out. I'm filled beyond capacity, stretching to the brink, ripping apart, and it feels so fucking good.

His hard cock relentless as he pistons into me. Throwing my legs over his shoulders and sliding to his knees in one smooth move, never once disconnecting, plunging harder and deeper. His hold on my hips so tight that I know I will have bruises on my bruises tomorrow. I don't care. The only thing on my mind right now is getting fucked thoroughly by this delicious god who has graced my life once again and is holding nothing back.

Total animalistic fucking.

My orgasm builds fast. I can't even believe my body is capable of coming again. I clamp down on his cock. His thrusts grow harder and faster, face strains with tension, veins popping in his neck, his cock reaching places inside me that I didn't even know I had.

I am panting and pulsating, my body tenses and everything shatters to pieces. My nails dig into his back, my legs tighten around his hips, the exquisite torture overtakes me.

"Ty!" My eyes roll back, time and sound cease to exist as I give myself over to the oblivion.

He thrusts one final time, pulling me tightly to him, head thrown back, and the most glorious roar emitting from his as he comes inside me. Rolling at the last moment so he's not collapsing on top of me.

My legs fall limply to the couch.

I'm done. Spent. Finished.

"Fuck, woman." He's breathing heavily. I like that I have that effect on him.

All I can manage in response is, "Mmhmm."

We lie there recouping and catching our breath until it returns to normal. He leaves for a moment, coming back with a warm wet cloth. He proceeds to clean me gently between the legs, before picking me up and carrying me into the bedroom. He throws back the covers and lies down, tucking me into him.

He puts his arm around my waist, hand cupping my breast. I'm so exhausted I can barely keep my eyes open.

"Stay with me?" I whisper, hoping it's not necessary to ask.

"Never leaving you again," he says, kissing my temple.

EPILOGUE

Genevieve

"You see this?" Ty tosses the day's newspaper on the kitchen table near my coffee. I'm feeding our daughter, Autumn, whose first birthday is today. "I'll take over," he says taking the small bowl and spoon from me. "Give it a read."

Autumn squeals in delight when Tyler takes my seat. He smiles big. "How's my girl? Ready for some sweet peas?"

She bangs her hands on the table in front of her, chanting, "Peas. Peas. Peas." Wiggling her bottom in her seat. She loves me, but she idolizes Ty. He's her entire world. That makes two of us.

We still get the newspaper, even though it's a seriously dying medium. I enjoy the feel of the paper in my hands and the ink on my fingers as I read it in the morning with my coffee. I grab the paper and stand next to him to read it.

ENTERTAINMENT NEWS

Creepy and Creepier to pen their own tall tale.
The pair, otherwise known as Eerie and Curious Daniels, have released a statement they are following in their late father's footsteps and have written a book. What they are calling a 'creative non-fiction' account of his death. The twins are currently serving twenty-year sentences for killing their father before attempting to frame their stepmother for the crime.
Their mother, Sarah Daniels, is serving her own ten-year sentence in a separate facility for attempting to cover up the crime. The Daniels twins are also serving concurrent five-year sentences for aggravated assault after locking their step-mother in a box and attempting to set her on fire. No release date for the book has been given.

"Well, that's interesting," I say after I finish. "Think they'll do it?"

"I think those two would do anything to keep their names in people's minds."

The press coined the girls "creepy and creepier" during their trial when neither showed any emotion about or remorse for the crime. Their bail was set at three-hundred seventy-five thousand dollars each. I was tempted to pay it. If only because it was Harrison's money, not mine, and I believe he would have done it had they killed someone else. But in the end, they were so nasty to me when I tried to visit them in jail, I opted against it. That was two years ago and in some ways, it still feels like yesterday. Ty has asked that we cut them from our lives completely and at this point, I'm okay with that.

I watch him as he scatters some puffs on the table for

Autumn to eat. This big, beautiful, burly man taking such care with his tiny daughter, it warms my heart every time I see it..

He proposed soon after Curious and Eerie were arrested with the same ring from so long ago. I was touched that he'd kept it. He was upset for a while because the diamond is about one-tenth the size of my ring from Harrison, but I couldn't love it more. It means more to me than anything I've ever been given in my life.

"What time are people getting here?" he asks, scooting his chair back and pulling me into his lap. He wraps his arms around my waist from behind, nuzzles my neck with his chin.

We're having a small party for Autumn today; she doesn't even realize it's her birthday even though we keep telling her. She'll have a good time even if the party ends up being more for us than her.

"Couple hours."

"What do I have to do?"

"Grill, be charming, keep the fridge stocked with beer."

We bought a house near the beach in Seaside that we could fix up, which Ty has been doing in his spare time. He's most proud of his outdoor kitchen, so anytime he gets the chance to grill, he's happy. He became a partner in his friend's security firm (from Seattle) and opened a division here that he runs with two guys working for him. And he's been slowly trying to accept the fact that maybe his brother did die from an accidental overdose, since he's yet to find proof otherwise; but it hasn't been easy.

"Autumn."

She looks up at him with a huge smile on her face. "Dada."

Ty chuckles. "You want to take a nap?"

She shakes her head vigorously.

"Not even for Daddy?"

More shaking.

"What if I say please?"

Erratic shaking that makes her baby fine blonde hair stick out at the ends.

"Daddy needs time with Mommy."

"No nap!" she cries.

I turn in his lap so I'm facing him, wrapping my arms around his neck. "She told you."

"I feel scolded and denied," he says, leaning in to capture my lips with his. A soft, lingering kiss that makes my toes curl.

"Poop!" Autumn announces, followed by a grunt.

Ty groans. "I got it." He lifts me off his lap, then sweeps her up from her chair and swings her down the hall toward her room, making airplane noises. She giggles the entire time, making me smile. Happiness has been a long time coming.

I ended up selling the three properties Harrison I shared together: the Lake Oswego, Seaside, and Seattle houses. I donated the proceeds to the children's literacy fund in Harrison's name.

I've also started a non-profit foundation for kids who want to write. We provide supplies, books, computers, mentors, even pens and paper if they want it; whatever a kid needs to get their imagination flowing. I'm proud of the work we do, and I think Harrison would be, too. It's a nice way to honor his name and make sure the ugliness surrounding his death doesn't taint it.

It keeps me busy but lets me set my own hours at the same time, which is perfect as a stay-at-home mom of (soon to be) two. Though Ty doesn't know it yet.

"Code brown," Ty yells from Autumns room. "We've got a blowout situation. Need to change her clothes too."

"I've got something for her to wear!" I yell back. Knowing the perfect shirt for her to wear, at least until people start arriving. I'll share the news with Ty, but I'm still wary of broadcasting it, since Autumn was my first successful, full-term pregnancy.

I bring the shirt I want him to dress her in.

He gets her changed, talking to her the whole time. "Mommy got a new shirt for the birthday girl." He stands her up on the changing table and she bounces in place. "Let's see what it says, 'Best big sister in the world.' Oh, that's cute isn't it, Autumn? You're the—"

He turns to me. "Wait. Are we . . . ?"

I nod, smiling.

He pulls me into a crushing hug with Autumn squished between us. "Don't know how you keep making my life better," he says, sniffling slightly. "But you do. Gonna spend my life tryin' to be worthy of it."

I lean in and kiss his neck just below his ear. "You already are babe. Ten times over." Because if there's one thing I learned in marrying and losing Harrison, it's that life rarely gives you second chances. It'll give you ups and downs and a ton of bullshit in between. But if you are one of the lucky ones to get that rare-as-fuck do-over, you better grab that opportunity by the horns and never look back. Live your life to its fullest, you only get it once.

THE END

Did you know that Ty's friend Mack has his own book? Check out Fearless, book one in the Agents and Assassins series - available now.

ACKNOWLEDGMENTS

This book just about killed me. Even as short as it is. I had to finish it coming off an unusually crazy busy time in my life, with a whole shit-load of obstacles in my way. Suffice it to say, I am so happy to be done. And so excited to share this with you!

I for sure could not have done it without the help of Rachel Radner. An amazing author and friend. Thank you for your constant support, guidance, and reassurance.

Amanda Shelley - thank you for giving me the chance to participate in this collaboration. I've enjoyed every part of it. Even the parts where I wanted to tell you I quit. (Insert smiley face here).

To all the authors collaborating in this project - thank you for the idea bouncing, the encouragement, and the community!

Krissy and Author Bunnies - totally saved my ass with your kick butt proofing skills - thank you!

Rachel Melignano - I hated you at times, going through the revisions, but you were right every time. I appreciate you, girl.

Remistimpson - I'm going to add this to the list of books you'll never read, but without whom I would never write. I love you.

BW - For as much as I made you inadvertently collaborate with me on this, you should be listed as a co-author. I heart you so much. I couldn't do anything that I do without you. I love you.

A final note - I was doing the final edits on this book as Roe v. Wade was overturned and everyone's worlds were rocked. I hated that I had a storyline with a terminated pregnancy already committed to paper. Which I attempted to handle with grace. That said, let it be known that I am a firm supporter of a woman's right to choose what happens with every single fucking cell that makes up her body. I am pro-choice all the way, regardless of the reason that makes a person have to choose. That choice should never be restricted, never taken away.

ABOUT THE AUTHOR

Denise has been reading since before she could talk. And to this day, escaping into a book is her go-to activity before anything else.

She likes to write about sassy women and semi-flawed alpha-esque men (hard on the outside and just a little soft on the inside.) Denise's female characters always have strong friendships, potty mouths, and like to drink—a lot.

Denise is loyal to a fault, a bit too sarcastic, blindingly optimistic, and pretty freakin' happy with life overall. If she couldn't be a writer, she'd be a singer in a classic rock band. Right after she learned to carry a tune. She has more purses than days in the month, an obsession with colored ink pens, and a slightly unhealthy bracelet habit.

Home is in the Pacific Northwest where she lives with six special needs Siberian Huskies and a husband (BW) who has the patience and tolerance of a saint. And, lest she forget, Denise also lives with too many to count characters inside her head, who will eventually have their stories told.

For more about Denise visit her website at: www.DeniseWells.com

If you want to know more about her books and new releases, join her newsletter list

Or follow her on any of the social media sites below.

facebook.com/denisewellsauthor

instagram.com/denisewellsauthor

bookbub.com/authors/denisewellsauthor

goodreads.com/denisewells

pinterest.com/denisewellsauthor

tiktok.com/@denisewellsauthor

patreon.com/DeniseWells

ALSO BY DENISE WELLS

Keeping Kat, a steamy second-chance firefighter romance

Romancing Remi, a steamy enemies to lovers romance

Loving Lexie, a steamy cowboy enemies to lovers romance

Seducing Sadie, a steamy firefighter romance

Trusting Tenley, an emotional second-chance at love romance

ANTHOLOGIES

High EX-Pectations, a romantic comedy short in the **Imperfect Date Anthology**

CAUGHT UNDER THE MISTLETOE - A Holiday Affair to Remember, a romantic comedy holiday short

STORYBOOK PUB CHRISTMAS WISHES - Mistle Oh-No, a romantic comedy holiday short

STORYBOOK PUB - Breezy Like Sunday Morning, a romantic comedy short

LIMITED RELEASES

GIRLS JUST WANNA HAVE FUNDAMENTAL RIGHTS - Charity Anthology

SEEDS OF LOVE A Charity Romance Anthology to benefit Ukraine - Charity Anthology

HOT AS F$#K SUMMER ROMANCE ANTHOLOGY - SULTRY SUMMER NIGHTS

LOCKED AND LOVED: An Isolated Romance Collection

SUMMER WITH YOU: Summer Shorts Collection

JUST A LICK Collection

LOVE LETTERS Collection

STOCKING STUFFERS Anthology

SNEAK PEEK OF OVERDRIVE

P rologue - the last eighteen months or so.

News Report

"DeeDee Wallace here with *Chasin' the Racin' News* coming to you live from the Los Angeles County Jail where racing superstar Jace Daughtry should be exiting at any moment. Unless you've been hiding under a rock, you know that Daughtry was arrested yesterday for allegedly stealing a car. I don't know about you, but the question I'm dying to ask is, doesn't he have access to enough cars already? I mean, you really gotta steal one?

Oh, here comes Jace and his attorney now. It looks like he's going to make a statement.

"I'm happy to report the Police have dropped all charges against Jace Daughtry in the case of the stolen car. It's been a tough twelve hours for my client, but justice has prevailed. We would appreciate that you respect his privacy at this time. We will not be taking questions. Thank you."

And I guess that's all they'll be saying today. Dave and Lisa, back to you in the studio.

News Report

"DeeDee Wallace here with *Chasin' the Racin' News* and have we got some news for you. A certain race champ favorite of mine was kicked out of a rock concert this past weekend after he was discovered *in flagrante delicto*. Jace Daughtry was caught with his pants down, literally, in the midst of receiving oral sex. Representatives from Daughtry's camp declined to comment on the issue. No arrests were made, just a slap on the wrist for the sexy racer. Maybe next time the mood strikes, he should use his wrist more, and in private, if you know what I mean.

News Report

"DeeDee Wallace here with *Chasin' the Racin' News* coming to you live from the Los Angeles County Jail. Jace Daughtry, the bad boy of racing, has found himself in the hotseat once again. This time for allegedly taking part in a bar brawl. Bar brawl. Try to say that ten times fast. He and his reps declined to comment as they left the building just moments ago. Lucky for the champ no charges were filed. But I'm pretty sure I saw some bandaged knuckles as Daughtry was escorted by his attorney to a waiting town car. I sure hope he has that guy on retainer and isn't paying by the incident at the rate he's going. Dave and Lisa, back to you in the studio.

News Report

"DeeDee Wallace here with *Chasin' the Racin' News* and have we got a story for you! Race champion Jace Daughtry has got a new addition to his crew. That's right folks, apparently our favorite racer didn't take his own advice to *wrap it before you tap it*. The bad boy spokesmodel for Gloves of Love is rumored to be the father of none other than supermodel Maralee Ackerman's brand new baby boy. Ackerman has confirmed that she gave birth to a baby boy two weeks ago and listed Jace Daughtry as the father on the birth certificate. Daughtry himself has been unavailable for comment, but his camp released a statement saying, *"Paternity has yet to be established. Mr. Daughtry will obviously make every effort to be an active and amicable participant in the mother and child's life should tests confirm he is the father."* All I'm saying is, with those two as parents, we can look forward to one beautiful baby.

CHAPTER ONE - JACE

Breakups are never pretty.

Especially when only one of you thought you were in a relationship to begin with. It doesn't matter what a guy says, if he's the one calling it quits, he's the villain. Plain and simple. At least right now I'm the villain over the phone instead of in person. Janice strikes me as the kind of lady to slap a guy when he's least expecting it. So I'm happy to be more than arm's length away.

I settle back in my custom-made Italian leather club

chair and take another sip of scotch while watching the sun setting beyond the Santa Monica shoreline. It's my favorite view in my house—the one that keeps me calm when I might otherwise be impatient and my voice soft instead of snapping.

"Janice, I'm sorry. I am. I thought I was clear from the beginning. I'm not that guy. I just can't do relationships." I keep my tone gentle. Trying to infuse as much regret into it as I can. Don't get me wrong, I'm not feeling regret, I just need Janice to think I am.

She continues crying. I lay the phone in my lap and turn on the speakerphone so I can simultaneously scroll through a few social media posts. I'm going to be traveling over my season break from racing and there are a few female friends I want to hit up in Thailand while I'm there. Throwing a few likes their way always helps to keep me at the forefront of their mind.

"Janice." I interrupt her sobs. "If I could be that guy, I would be him be with you." Because if there's one thing I know how to do, it's how to let a woman down gently.

"I know you've had *issues* in the past. But that was then, and this is now." She sniffles. "I thought it was different with us."

"I wish it was, babe." That's not true, what I really wish is that I could hang up the phone. But that would be career suicide.

There's a reason they say don't shit where you eat.

Janice runs South Coast Media, the PR firm that handles my racing career. I race cars for a living. A fucking fantastic living I might add. She handles a few of the guys on the circuit as well as celebrities in other professions. She's used to high-profile clients and what that lifestyle entails.

She's also known to *date* her younger clientele. And by

date, I mean sleep with. I can't fault her for that. She's a beautiful woman, an ex-model from Colombia, who has kept her youthful looks and tight figure with the help of both science and genetics. But if you haven't guessed already Janice is also a cougar, and I went drunkenly into her den. For what I thought would be a quick romp. A one —maybe two—and done. Somehow it turned into a few weeks.

What can I say?

She made sure it was convenient and easy. Until it wasn't. Once she started automatically adding herself as my 'plus one' no matter the event—not as PR, as my date—I recognized there was a problem and I'm putting an end to it.

There's convenient and easy. And then there's clingy and complicated.

Convenient girls equal awesome.

Clingy girls equal awful.

She's still sniffling.

And talking.

"If you wish it was different, then just make it that way," she says.

I don't remember now what she's referring to, too lost in my own thoughts to think back on the conversation. No matter, my response won't change.

"I'm sorry, Janice. I really am. I have to be true to myself and that just wouldn't be me. I'm not that guy."

It's a canned line of bullshit. I know it. She must know it. Hell, anyone who hears it knows it. But, let's be honest, what are you supposed to do? You can't just tell a girl the truth.

Hey, babe, you're getting too attached, gotta cut you loose.

That never goes over well. There's no alternative to spewing bullshit.

Breakups already aren't pretty. Add honesty into the mix

and you better be at Defcon 5 readiness, 'cause shits about to go down. A woman will tell you, you got to be real—yes, like the Cheryl Lynn song (don't judge, I have a slight disco addiction)—that she wants you to share your thoughts and feelings. But she's lying.

That's not what she wants to hear. And if you don't tell her what she wants to hear, she'll make up excuses for why and try to stick around longer. So, why not just make up the excuse for her? Save us all a bunch of time.

If the '*I'm not that guy*' line doesn't work, then I just tell them one of three things.

1. I'm not in the right head space for a relationship.

2. I have too much baggage to be a good partner for anyone.

3. I need time to work on myself. It's me, not you.

Women eat that shit up. Especially '*it's me, not you.*' They pretend they don't. But any time a woman can walk away believing that if there was a '*the one*' it would be them, and the problem is you not them, they'll take that flimsy excuse check all the way to the bank and cash it.

Case in point:

"Janice, I need to be honest with you," I tell her.

She immediately stops crying. Her ears perk up and she holds her breath—at least that's what I imagine happens on the other end of the phone line—waiting to hear my truth.

"You're too good for me, Janice. Deep down you know I'm not worthy of someone like you, and I don't want you to settle. You're going to find a guy who is, and he'll be the luckiest son-of-a-bitch around. A guy who will treat you like the queen you are."

"What if I don't want to be treated like a queen?" She hiccups.

"Why wouldn't you?"

"Because I just want you." The blubbering starts anew. I've got to end this soon. I'm not sure how much more I can take.

"You don't want me, Janice. You want the idea of me. The one you've created in your mind. The real me is a piece of shit."

"No, you're not."

A woman will always argue that point, and you have to move past it without seeming too artificial. The number of examples I could give her for times I've been a piece of shit to women is well into the double digits. I'm sure a therapist would tell me it has more to do with being abandoned by my mother as a child than anything else. But I'm pretty sure I'm a piece of shit to everyone in my life. Except maybe for my best friend, West, who also happens to be my crew-chief.

I let Janice sit for a moment with her thoughts before continuing. Eventually, she'll realize I'm right.

I hope.

"I need to know that we can still be friends after this, Janice. And that it won't impact our working relationship."

"Of course not," she snips. "What kind of person do you think I am?"

"A professional first, Janice. I also think you're a professional first."

I say that more for her than anyone. Not that I think she needs reminding.

That's not true; I definitely think she needs reminding.

She has the power to tank my career if she wants to. So, I need to make sure that doesn't happen by any means possible.

I've got two months left on my season break. My goal is to find and fuck as many different women as I can. This whole *sleeping with one woman for the sake of convenience* bullshit is just that. Bullshit. To keep my privacy, and ability to follow through with my sexual freedom, I tell Janice I'm heading out of town for the rest of my break until the season begins to ramp up again. That I need to clear my head and work on myself. And that I'll call her as soon as I return.

It's a lie, I have no intention of doing any of those things. My head is clear, I've learned my lesson. If something seems too easy, too good to be true, it's 'cause it fucking is. But telling her those things is what she wants to hear. I'm nothing if not consistent. Plus, it's time for this guy to cool his engines for a while.

GET YOUR COPY OF OVERDRIVE HERE - FREE ON KU

9 781960 421029